Falafel and Fatalities:
Alphabet Soup Mysteries

Book 6

Erica J Whelton

Publisher: Sunseri Design Publishing
Cover Designer: Mariah Sinclair Book Cover Design
ISBN: 978-1-956069-33-4

Printed in the United States of America

To Elaine Davis.
You are an angel on Earth!!
Thank you for all your help

Chapter One

I woke with a start. It took a second to realize it was just the giggles and squeals of Ivy and Dove as Shayla herded them upstairs to her bathroom to get ready for school. Today was the first day back after the winter break.

We were still trying to adjust to having the little girls living here. When Shayla had moved in with us, she had been fairly self-sufficient. However, Ivy and Dove were only eight years old, so they needed a lot of care and guidance.

I grabbed my phone. There was a text from Kyle Rafferty.

Raff: **Good morning, beautiful. Have a good day.**

We'd been dating for almost two months, but it felt longer because I'd known him since middle school. It was new and familiar at the same time. Like starting on the fifth date, instead of the first.

And now that I was back in my hometown after years of traveling, we saw each other often.

He was a police officer with the Dashwood Police Department. That meant, while I was investigating murders, a task I'd started doing to clear my name, we ran into each other at the crime scenes. He was also the responding officer a few times when I'd gotten into trouble.

To think where our relationship is now. I chuckled at the thought.

I then typed out my reply to him with a good morning. He would likely not see it until later. For me, getting those texts each morning always puts a smile on my face.

I stretched, then thought about the day ahead. Dread settled into my stomach as I remembered what today was.

It was the day of the local memorial for Samir Saad, the owner and chef at the Spicy Fig. It was being held at Caruso's Funeral Home, and I'd heard it was going to be packed.

The family had just returned from Lebanon after taking his body home to be buried. Several local restaurant owners wanted to have a memorial for him. They'd done all the organizing and just invited the family as honored guests.

I ran downstairs to start breakfast before the girls had to get to school. Blueberry pancakes and homemade sausage were their new favorite thing, and I could whip them up fairly quickly. I made the sausage in advance, so I had it on hand when needed.

I had the batter mixed, and the sausage cooked when I heard the girls heading down the stairs.

"Good morning, Jess!" Ivy and Dove said.

They were smiling brightly with a healthy glow about them. Much like their big sister, Shayla, they had a rough start to life. Not always having enough food, hot water, or clothing.

When they first arrived, they were shy and unsure. They also had a pale, almost sickly look about them. It was so good to see the transformation in all three of them.

In just a few weeks, they were thriving and happy. Good nutrition and cleanliness went a long way. Plus, they weren't abused and neglected any longer.

"Good morning, girls. Did you sleep well?"

"I did," Ivy said.

"Me too."

"Good. You have all your homework in your bag?" I asked as I plated the first pancakes. One on a plate for each girl.

Even though it had been during Christmas break, they had to read each day and keep track of what and how long they read. It was something new to me, but thankfully both enjoyed reading so it was a fun thing we did daily, even on weekends and over the break.

"I do."

"Me too."

"Good."

"Morning, Jess," Shayla said, coming down finally.

She was dressed for work and would drop her sisters off at school on the way to her new job.

After losing their mother a few months ago and with the twins' father in prison and their paternal grandmother being charged with conspiracy to commit murder, Shayla had gotten custody of the twins. That meant she had to work hours more suitable to their schedule then what I had to offer.

She had worked for me until graduating high school in December and winning the 41st Annual Culinary Arts High School Competition. Unfortunately, I only had an evening shift position open at this time, but if a day shift became available, she had an open invite to return.

However, her win had provided a lot of opportunities for her, and she had job offers coming from just about every place in town, making it a tough decision.

However, the one she ultimately accepted was from Honey's Sweet Treats. The owner, Honey, was a local bee farmer and ran the cake shop. She offered all kinds of pastries and cakes.

It was the perfect place for Shayla as they opened at eight in the morning and closed by four. Plus, Shay was a pastry chef and had a natural talent for baking.

It meant she could take the girls to school, and I would pick them up. I'd watch them for an hour or so until Shayla got home. My job was making snacks and supervising homework.

"Good morning. Pancake?" I offered.

"Just coffee," she mumbled as she made a beeline for the coffee pot.

"Didn't sleep well?" I asked.

She had been having trouble sleeping lately. With the care of her sisters and her own future to think about, it was a lot to worry about, especially at only eighteen.

"A little better but not great."

"Sorry, Shay," Ivy mumbled.

"Me too."

"Don't worry. I'm fine." She smiled at them. "Are y'all almost done eating?"

"I want another pancake," Dove said.

"I like the sausage."

"Okay, but hurry. We need to get going soon, and you both still need to brush your teeth and put on your shoes." She gave them each a little more breakfast, then turned to me. "Are y'all closing to go to Samir's memorial?"

"We are. Is Honey closing shop too?"

"No, we have some custom orders being picked up during that time, but she said if I want to go, she'll stay behind."

"So, are you going?"

She looked at her sisters. "I'm not sure. I want to pay my respects, but ..." She put a gentle hand on Ivy's head.

She didn't need to finish her thought. I knew exactly what she meant. She'd had enough with death and sadness. Me too, but I was going anyway, especially since the family had extended a personal invitation to me.

The girls finished their breakfast.

"I'll get everything cleaned up for you," I told Shayla.

"Thanks!" She smiled. "Okay, ladies, upstairs. Brush teeth then shoes, and out the door."

She chased the girls upstairs and a few minutes later, they came pounding back down, along with Vee, the cutest postal worker.

"Bye, Jess! Bye, Vee!"

"Bye, bye! Bye, bye!"

I waved. "See y'all after school."

"Thanks, Jess. Bye, Vee," Shayla smiled. "Don't run in the street!" I heard her say as the door shut behind her.

"They're a handful, but so cute," Vee chuckled, taking a seat at the island. "Anything left?"

"Yep, I saved some just for you." I put a plate in front of her.

"You're the best."

"Oh, I know."

We laughed, then I began cleaning up while she ate.

"Are you going to the memorial?" I asked her.

"I'm gonna try. Not sure if I'll be able to leave or not."

"It sounds like a lot of people are going to be there."

"Yeah, I've been hearing the buzz." She took a bite of pancake, chewing slowly before asking me the million-dollar question. "Are you going to look into his death?"

Everyone knew what I had been doing, and it wouldn't surprise me if I got pulled into this one. The media had nicknamed me the crime-fighting chef.

Even though I had now helped with five cases, I was still reluctant to get involved. I have no reason to, but Samir and his family had become good friends in the short time I'd known them.

Never say never, I thought.

"Oh, gosh. I know people are probably going to expect me to, but it's been a few weeks, if they haven't found the killer, it is only going to get harder. You know clues get colder and people get close-lipped."

"That's true, but you've got me, I can help."

"This case is going to be challenging due to the lack of substantial evidence."

"Yeah, but that hasn't stopped you before."

"I know, but there is nobody here any longer. What if we need it?"

The police and medical examiner's office had released him to his family as they felt they'd got all they could. Once he was cleared and with the restaurant closed until further notice, the family had taken his body to Lebanon to be buried.

"Ask Rafferty what they do have?"

"You know that Raff and I agreed not to talk about any cases, but from the small bit we had discussed, they didn't have any leads and limited physical evidence. Only some grainy security footage and the bullet from Samir's chest. There was no forced entry, and no murder weapon found on sight."

"But the media is reporting it as a robbery, so likely some kid from James Street looking for drug money," Vee said.

"I think if it were, the police would report it as such. My feeling is there was something more to it, but still, I don't want to get involved."

"See? You have to do it. You have an instinct for this stuff, and my offer to help still applies."

"You have been an awesome help, but I just can't keep investigating murders, can I?"

"Why not? The restaurant is doing so well, better than you expected and you now have more time away from it."

"That's true."

There were now four of us that rotated as executive chef, and we were training a new line cook to be a fifth in the future. That would allow me to step even further back and mostly be just the owner or work on other projects.

"Well, I better get out of here. I'll see you either at the service or later this evening." She rinsed up her plate, then waved as she went out the door.

I stood there in the now quiet house. I didn't have to work today, but I would go in just to check in and talk to my manager. We would be closing at one today to allow anyone wanting to go to the service time to do so. We would then open back up at four.

With the kitchen cleaned, I went to shower and dress for the day.

An hour later, I was walking into the bustling kitchen of my restaurant. It had been open for nine months or so, and it still took my breath away. This really happened. I really opened my own restaurant, and it was actually successful.

That was my biggest fear, and, to my surprise, it was working. People loved it. Noah, my manager, said it was me they loved, but I think the awesome food helped a lot. Plus, I had an amazing staff.

"Hey, Chef!"

"Hey, I didn't think you'd be here today."

"Looking good, Chef."

They started yelling when they saw me. I greeted them all, checking stations, and smelling the soup. Minestrone today.

"Smells good." I smiled at Hannah.

"Thanks. I learned from the best."

"Ha, I don't know about that. You were pretty well trained when you got here but thank you."

"Hey, I thought I heard you," Noah said coming from the office. "What are you doing here?"

"Just thought I would check on things."

"Worried about closing at 1?"

"You know me too well." I chuckled. "Any push back online?"

Cullen, the assistant manager and social media manager, had posted about our closing online. If the customers were upset, they would definitely let us know. Like recently, we didn't have my famous alphabet soup. I thought they were going to show up with pitchforks and torches, but we made a batch, and things settled down. I would never make that mistake again.

"Oh, I remember the soup incident," he said with a laugh.

"Me too. Hence the reason I'm here. No more soup incidents."

"I haven't even looked yet."

"Me neither. I wanted moral support when I did."

"Well, let's go check together."

A few other employees greeted me as we made our way to the office. He was already logged into the computer, so he went to our first social media app.

"Are you ready?"

"No, but yeah."

He pulled it up. I held my breath as I read the first comments.

Samir was a good soul.

He will be missed.

Prayers for the family.

We understand. Prayers.

"Oh, these aren't bad. I was worried for nothing." I read one that said they would miss us being open, but they would come early. That was as negative as it got.

"You were worried about nothing," he laughed.

"It hasn't always been for nothing. You remember the group that was trying to sabotage me, right?"

It was a group of four, two of them worked for me. They were holding a grudge against my father for killing theirs. I had nothing to do with it, but they didn't care. They just wanted to take someone down. My father was serving his time in prison, what more did they want?

"True, true."

"Has anyone said they were going today?"

"Almost everyone. Marco has an appointment at the VA and Ava has to pick up her kids. There may be a few others that can't make it, but they are the only ones I know about."

"Well, good. I want us to have a large show of support for them."

"He was one of the good ones," Noah said. "So, are you hanging out until 1?"

"No, I have some errands to run. I want to go talk to Honey about an order and then talk to Tina about the art festival."

"Are we going to do a booth?"

"I'm thinking about it."

"Nice. People will love that."

"Well, I'll see ya later."

"See ya."

Chapter Two

I parked in the crowded parking lot at Caruso's Funeral Home. It was good to see this place so full. As I climbed out of the car, I saw a familiar face a few cars down.

"Hey, Jen."

"Hey, Jess!" She walked over, hugging me. "It's a shame about Samir, huh?"

"Yes, it is. Have you heard anything?"

"Not at all, but I figured you would with a cop as a boyfriend." She nudged me slightly.

"Ha, yeah, you'd think, but no."

"How are things with mister tall and sexy?"

"It's going well, but kind of weird."

"Because you knew him before he learned about deodorant?"

"Yep," I said with a chuckle. "What is it with middle-school boys and deodorant? But actually, it feels weird because it feels like we are starting further along in the relationship, and yet, it is still new."

"That's good, though, right?"

I thought about my bad luck in dating, and yes, things with Kyle Rafferty were much, much better than any other relationship I'd been in. He wasn't trying to use me, belittle me, or ghost me. It was real and he was a good guy.

"Yeah, it's good."

We stepped into the crowded building, making our way through the attendees. It was good to see so many here to honor the Saad family. Jen went to stand with some of her staff.

I also saw some of my employees were already here. They were huddled together against a wall. They waved or nodded in greeting. I waved back, then glanced around trying to find the family. Instead, I saw Nathan, from Beaks and Brews.

"Hey, Jess. Good to see you."

"Oh, hey, Nathan. Good to see you, too."

"How's business?"

"Good, good. How about you?"

"People love chicken." He chuckled.

"You know I do!"

"Yeah, you need to come by soon."

"I will." I looked around. "Do you know if the family is here?"

"Fatima and Anwar? Yeah, they are in that room." He pointed behind us. "There is a nice memorial set up with pictures and things."

"Great. I want to go pay my respects to them."

I waved as I fought my way to the door. Stepping into the room, there was soft music playing, a light scent on the air, and the lights were lowered. It was less crowded with only a few chairs occupied.

I remembered being here not long ago for Shayla, Ivy, and Dove's mother's funeral. Little did I know that day how much life would change.

Fatima was seated near the front of the room. Anwar was standing to her right. A younger woman was seated next to her, holding Fatima's hand. Then a young man standing on the other side of her. He looked awkwardly around, fidgeting with his hands.

This would be the first time I had spoken to them in person since his passing. I took a deep breath. I stepped forward, bending over so I was closer to her eye level.

"Hi, Fatima. I'm so sorry for your loss."

"Thank you, Chef Jessica," she said. "He thought a lot of you and would be happy you came."

"He was one of the good guys, for sure. The world is not going to be the same without him."

She made a slight sobbing sound, but didn't cry. Instead, she took a deep breath.

"He thought that way. He had a big personality for sure," she said, looking up at me. "Oh, have you met my whole family? I think you only know Anwar." She gestured.

"I don't think I have." I stood to greet them.

"This is my baby, Ayman. I believe he was in school with Shayla."

"Oh, yes, she mentioned him. Hi, Ayman."

He mumbled something that sounded like nice to meet you but kept his eyes down.

"This is my daughter, Mona. She's a nurse at the hospital and then, of course, you know Anwar."

"Yes, nice to meet you, Mona and good to see you, Anwar."

"You're going to find his killer, right?" Anwar snapped. "They call you the crime-fighting chef for a reason, no?"

Fatima and Mona gasped. Ayman smirked, but Anwar stared unblinking at me.

"Um, uh, yeah, I'm going to try, but now is not the time to discuss," I said without thinking. Decision made; I was going to do this. "Maybe we can set up some time to discuss this later?"

"No, we need to talk about it now. You have found killers for others, so why not us? Huh? Huh?"

"Why me though? Why not the police? It's their job," I argued.

"You have something against us, then, is that it?"

"Anwar! That's enough. Jess has already said she'd help, but you badger her so, she isn't going to want to." Fatima took my hand. "I will come talk to you in a few days. Okay?"

"Yes. Again, I'm sorry for your loss." With that, I turned and went back into the main hall.

I wasn't going to be berated by Anwar. It was likely his fault that his father was dead, given his shady business dealings recently.

Calm down, Jess, I thought. *He is grieving. Sometimes it comes out as anger.*

I chatted with a few of the other chefs. We swapped kitchen war stories. There were a lot of laughs, until one of the line cooks from Mills chimed in.

"What do you know? You're a TV chef."

"Ah, give her a break, Jess is a grinder," Jen said, punching him in the arm.

"Yeah, man, you don't want to go up against Jessica," Nathan said.

"She didn't beat me, but mad respect to her anyway," Kano said with a laugh. I laughed along with him.

No, I didn't beat him when we'd gone head-to-head in a hometown themed competition. He would never let me live it down.

"Thanks, y'all. But to answer, I did work in kitchens too. I wasn't just on television."

"It would be fun if someday they would come film here," Kano said.

"Yeah, we have a lot of great chefs here in Dashwood," Nathan said.

"Who do we talk to?" Jen asked. They all looked at me.

"What? What do you think I can do?"

"You have got to still have connections, right?" Jen said.

"I don't any longer, but, um, let me think about it and see what I can do."

Anwar came walking through, we locked eyes. His face changed to a stoic scowl. The stony expression sent chills through me. What had I done to him?

He broke eye contact then continued walking through the room as a few people tried to talk to him, but he barely acknowledged them. I guess it wasn't personal. He was just a dick.

"What's his problem?" someone close by asked.

"He's a douche," someone else said.

"He lost his father. I doubt I'd be Mr. Personality if I'd lost my dad," another person answered.

"True, true."

"Fair enough."

Hearing them voice my own thoughts, I knew they were right. I decided to give him a pass on his poor manners with me. Still if you ask someone for help, shouldn't you be polite?

Shortly after, they called everyone into the other room. One by one, people got up to say a few words about Samir.

Anwar stood against the wall listening arms crossed tightly over his chest, though the rest of the family seemed to enjoy hearing the stories about Samir. They laughed and cried along with the audience as story after story was shared.

Then it was my turn. I walked to the podium at the front of the room. I was just steps from the family. I nodded with a flat smile at them as I took my spot.

"Hello all. For those that don't know me, I'm Chef Jessica, Jess to my friends. I own the Crock Pot restaurant." There were some claps and cheers. "Thank you. I didn't know Samir long, but he always had a quick smile, a warm greeting, and a plate of falafels with my name on it." Laughs from the crowd.

"Samir, I will truly miss your stories and your welcome spirit. You will be missed by all who knew you and those that didn't have truly missed out on a warm friend. Until we meet again." I bowed my head, then stepped away from the podium.

"Thank you, Jess," I heard Fatima say as I walked passed her. I smiled at her briefly before taking my seat.

The last of the speakers spoke, and then I had to get out of here so I could pick up the little girls. I said goodbye to those around me, then walked out.

In the parking lot, I was stopped just feet from my car.

"Chef Jessica," Anwar sneered. "Now that my mother isn't here to chide me, I do expect you to find my father's killer." His voice was like a hiss as he stepped close to me. Too close.

I took a step back. "As I've said, I will try."

"You better!" He pointed a shaky finger at my face. "You owe my father."

"Owe him for what?"

He stared at me. "He was an elder, smart, and a pillar in this community! Just look at what all those people in there had to say. He's owed respect."

"Um, okay."

He walked away briskly then. I stood there frozen. That was an odd interaction. Not sure why all the pay of respect fell to my shoulders, but I wasn't going to stand here arguing with him. It would get me nowhere and right now I had to get across town to the school.

Plus, he was already back in the building, so it wasn't like he had given me a chance to argue.

The crowd started moving out of the funeral home into the parking lot. People were clustering around chatting or getting into their own cars, meaning my window to get out of the parking lot easily was closing. I quickly strode the last feet to my car.

Putting the car in gear, I slowly maneuvered around groups of people or other cars as we snaked through the parking lot to the exit.

Finally, success. I was on my way to get the girls.

Looking in my rearview at the funeral home, a chill ran through me as I remembered Anwar's cold energy. He creeped me out.

Chapter Three

I plated two Dijon chickens with mashed potatoes and asparagus, then slid them into the pickup window. Then I started on the chicken fried steak plate. It had been like this most of the day, order after order. It made me happy.

One of my first restaurant jobs out of high school had been at a slow business that barely had this many orders all day. After several months of struggling to stay afloat, they closed.

I had learned a lot of lessons on what not to do. The owner had tried to cut corners with cheap food products. The Executive Chef was short-tempered, which led to an unhappy kitchen staff. The rest of the employees weren't trained well. They didn't put orders in correctly, which caused unhappy customers.

There were a few others but that one had been the worst. I noted every one of their mistakes and took them as lessons.

"Chef, Fatima Saad is here," Ava said, coming over to my station.

"Is Anwar with her?"

"No, she's alone. I got her a drink and a basket of biscuits and corn muffins. She declined a menu."

Thank goodness. I didn't want to deal with him.

"Okay, I'll be a minute or two."

I was the only chef today, but my line cook Eli could take over for a few minutes. He wasn't quite as fast as he needed to be for executive chef, but he was getting better each day. Opportunities like this would help him.

"I got you, Chef," he said, coming to take over.

"I just have this one left." I pointed to the ticket. "And this one is... done." I put the green beans next to the chicken fried steak and put the plate in the pickup window, just as Marco came to grab orders. He smiled as he carried them away.

"Got it, Chef."

I headed straight to the sink to wash. I cringed when I caught my reflection. After washing my hands and face, I pulled the scarf off my head, trying to smooth my hair down. Shoving the scarf in my pocket, I headed to the dining area, stopping first by the bar to grab a glass of peach iced tea.

I saw they had seated Fatima in a quiet corner booth.

"Hi, Fatima. May I?" I gestured to the opposite side of the booth.

"Yes, please, join me." She smiled. "Thank you for seeing me today. I had to sneak away. Anwar is not happy."

I bit my tongue but wanted to ask if he ever was.

"I'm sure he is struggling."

"You're so kind, but I know what kind of person he is. Spoiled, feels entitled, and thinks the world owes him. For what? I have no idea. I didn't raise him that way, or so I thought." She sighed. "Perhaps we did. He was doted on. More so than the other two. He was the oldest and a son. It happened."

I thought about that. It made sense. He probably had been raised to think he deserved more and better treatment. I saw it with my own brothers and my cousin, Sully Junior. They acted just like Anwar.

Even as sweet as Vee was, sometimes she didn't understand the world. She had been raised with a softer hand, a softer place to land, and it made her expect certain treatment. It didn't mean she was wrong or even my brothers, cousin or Anwar were wrong. They had just been set up to think differently.

"I can understand." I smiled at her. "So, do you have any information for me about his killer?"

"I brought you a copy of the security footage." She slid a USB drive across to me.

I fought the urge to laugh at our interaction. If anyone was watching us, what would they think? Some espionage going on, maybe?

"Thanks. This will help. Other than this, is there anything you can tell me? What was he doing up there at that time of night?"

"Well, we had been receiving threats for a few weeks leading up to this and then the alarms kept going off. He'd go to check, but nothing was there, or he'd see someone running away, but never any damage or anything. He thought it was just some kids." She took a deep breath. "Then that night he arrived and someone was waiting. When Samir entered, they were seated in a chair holding a gun right at him. They talked for several minutes before ... you know, before they shot him."

"Is that what this shows?"

"Yes," she said, her voice cracking.

"I thought I kept hearing robbery was the motive, no?" I asked it, even though I really did have my doubts about that. With no other ideas, I thought I'd see what she said.

"That's what the police want people to think. It makes them feel safer than organized crime," she said.

"Oh."

"Yeah, this is the stuff people don't talk about. I think it was because Anwar made some bad deals, and they came to collect."

"Could that be why he's so angry?" I asked.

"Ah, perhaps, or guilt," she looked around. "His entitled attitude led him into making such a bad deal. He felt he deserved certain success and thought that was the way to get it. The easy way, the fastest way. He didn't want to work for anything."

"And you have no information about who this person was, or I mean, what group they are with?" I had no idea what to call it. Gang? Mob? Organization? I don't know.

"Not really and Anwar doesn't know. He works with a management company, but they are so well padded that you can't find out who owns them. The police have been digging, but everything on paper is legal."

I had never heard of that before. Was it really a thing? I suddenly wanted to have a conversation with Rafferty. Though I knew he couldn't tell me, even if he knew. Still, maybe he had some ideas about the organized crime in Dashwood.

"And you're sure that they were coming to collect?"

"Yes, well, almost sure." She dropped her hands into her lap. "No, I honestly don't know. We don't know what was said since there isn't audio."

"Was there anyone else who would have a reason to kill him?"

She fidgeted in the seat, scanning the dining room. She lowered her voice as she leaned closer.

"Back in the 1980s, Samir had been involved in some secret military operations. They were in partnership with a few other countries. I don't know the details because we had only just gotten married then. Things went wrong and the US relocated us to the

United States for our protection. We were given different names and started a brand new life here."

"Wow, and would anyone from then know how to find you?"

"I don't know. I honestly don't think so, but it could be possible. I mean anything is possible."

"And you told the police about this?"

She looked down at her hands. "No. I only thought about it last night."

"You should probably call Detective Upton."

"Do you think he would want to know this?" she asked.

"Yes, I do. If you think there is any chance that someone from his past could be coming after him, the police will want to know." Though to me that sounded like it was too long ago, but she seemed to think it was possible.

"Okay, I'll call him later."

I needed to get back to work, but I didn't want to rush her either.

"Did they mention any fingerprints or forensic evidence?"

"No, no. They said no prints, footprints, or anything like that. The bullet was untraceable. I didn't even know you could trace bullets."

I nodded. "Is there anything else you can think of?"

"No, that's all I can think of."

"Okay, well, if you think of anything else that can help, please feel free to reach out, and please call Detective Upton about what you told me."

"I will and thank you Jess. Samir trusted you. He had told me days before that if anything happens to him, to talk to you. You would know what to do."

"Um, oh, wow. I don't know what to say." No pressure or anything, but a dead man thought I could find his killer.

"I will let you get back to work. Bless you, dear."

We stood, she got on tiptoe to kiss my cheeks, then squeezed my hands before turning to leave. I watched her tiny figure go out the door.

I had no idea if I was prepared to take on organized crime, but if Samir had requested it, I was going to try. I turned the USB drive over and over in my hand. This held a small key to the murderer, but thinking about watching the moment he was killed did not sound appealing.

I'd just watch up to that point to see what it shows. Then I'd try to talk to Rafferty tonight, if I got a chance.

I got back to work, but that USB drive was burning a hole in my pocket.

When Parker arrived for his shift, I ran to the office, pulling the USB out of my pocket. I needed to watch it here because I didn't know what it would show. I couldn't take a chance of the little girls seeing it by accident.

"Wanna watch something with me?" I asked Noah.

"Always." He spun around in the chair. "What is it?"

"The security footage from the Spicy Fig."

"Oh, from the night?"

"Yep."

"Is that why Fatima was here?"

"Yes, it is. She did warn me it is difficult to watch, so I don't want to watch it alone."

"What are we watching?" Cullen said, coming in the office for his evening shift.

"Oh, hey, footage from the Spicy Fig."

"Oh, dang." He took a seat in the third chair. "Alrighty, I'm in."

I pulled up the video, looking at my friends' faces for confirmation. My heart was thumping as I hit play.

The screen was dark with just light coming from the lights on the street. A shadow walks to the center of the restaurant and sits in a chair. The shadow is tall, lean, but there are no features to tell if it is a male or female. There were no distinguishing features to identify the person.

They stayed there for quite a while without moving much. Then a light turns on, but it must be in the kitchen as the dining area is still dark. It casts strange shadows around the room and onto the stranger, making it even more difficult to see his face.

Samir walks into the frame confronting the stranger. They argue, but the stranger holds the gun, saying something that causes Samir to take a seat. The strangers looks as if they are talking, but without sound, it is hard to tell what is happening.

"Should we turn it off before … oh!" I said, as we saw Samir jerk back and then fall to the floor. The stranger walks over, pushes him with his foot, then spits before walking out.

"What the hell?" Noah said. "What was that spitting about?"

"It looks like whoever this is, they have a real beef with him." Cullen added.

"It's horrible. I hope that the family didn't watch that part," I mumbled.

"I'm sure they did. That shot comes out of nowhere," Noah said.

"If we could hear what they were saying, maybe it wasn't unexpected," Cullen said.

Noah and I looked at him. I couldn't disagree with him, but this whole thing made me sad.

"So, what do y'all think about this?"

"You want to know if we have any ideas who this is?" Cullen asked.

"Or a motive?"

"I guess both."

"No idea."

"Yep, I have never seen this person before."

I sighed. "Well, thanks. I'm glad I watched this here and not at home with the girls." I checked the time. "Oh, bleep! I'm going to be late picking them up. Gotta go." I grabbed the USB and my stuff, waving as I ran out of the office.

Chapter Four

The girls were waiting patiently for me, talking to another little girl when I pulled up. I was only a few minutes late, but it made me smile to see them looking so relaxed and happy after all they had been through.

"Bye, Anya!" the girls yelled as they climbed in.

"Bye, Ivy. Bye-bye, Dove!"

"Sorry I'm a little late."

"No, you are on time. Anya's mom is late."

"Yeah, so we got to play with her while we waited."

"Well, how was school?"

They began talking at the same time both to me and to each other. I couldn't follow half of what they were telling me. Something about a little boy during library time. He wouldn't sit still, so he had to go to the office.

Then they both had different stories about their day. Ivy wanted to tell me all about recess and her friends, while Dove was focused on music class and the songs they are learning.

I just listened to and enjoyed the moment with the little girls who came bursting into my life at a low moment in theirs. They have quickly become my favorite part of my life. I would be sad if one day Shayla moved away taking her sisters with her.

When we arrived home, I went into the kitchen to get their snack.

"Slices of apple and some cheese slices?" I asked them.

"Yes!" they yelled.

They had never had it, but it quickly became their favorite. It had always been my favorite too. Something Auntie Rita had taught me when I was just a little kid.

"Okay, go put your shoes away, wash your hands, then it should be ready by the time you get back." I grabbed two apples and a block of cheddar cheese. I made quick work of cutting the fruit and a few slices from the block of cheese.

The girls came running back laughing. I loved that they had settled into being kids again. When I was young, it had taken me a few years to get over my father being arrested and taken away in front of me.

Granted, I didn't have a sibling to help me forget and I had watched a man die. Shot by my father, so a little different situation. Still, I was happy to see Ivy and Dove settled into their new life.

"Did you wash up?"

"Yes!"

"No, you didn't." Dove pointed at Ivy.

"I did so. You didn't."

"Did either of you?"

They giggled, then ran off again, back to the half bathroom. I could hear them splashing and giggling.

"Done!" They came back holding their damp hands for my inspection.

I laughed, grabbing a hand towel to dry their hands better.

"Okay, snack and then homework," I said. They dug in while I asked them about school and friends. They were very chatty, and I loved it.

"What's for dinner?" Dove asked around her last bite of apple.

"How are you still hungry?" I laughed.

"She *always* thinks about food," Ivy teased, as she made silly faces at her sister.

"So do you!"

"Yeah, we never had such good food," Ivy said, with Dove nodded rapidly beside her.

That made me sad. Everyone should have good food, but perhaps that was just my chef's heart thinking that.

"Well, how do y'all feel about a creamy, cheesy, beefy pasta?" It was a quick and easy dish that could feed a crowd. It was one of the first meals I'd made for them, and they asked for it once a week since.

"With salad?"

"And bread?"

"Yep."

"Yay!"

"I love it!" Dove cheered. "Okay, I am going to get all my homework done fast."

"Me too."

They ran to grab their backpacks to begin. While they were occupied, I told them I was going upstairs to change my clothes.

When I came back down, Vee had arrived home and was giggling away with the twins.

"What is going on here? Are you distracting them from their homework?" I laughed.

"Of course, that's what a fun auntie does!" Vee said.

"So, I am making that cheesy beef pasta with salad and bread tonight."

"Oh, that sounds good, but I have a date."

The girls giggled at her words.

"Ew, Auntie Vee has a date."

"With a boy?"

"Yes, with a boy," she told them.

"Elias?" I asked.

Elias was the owner of a tire shop and tow company in town. We had gone to school with him, and they had reconnected a couple of months ago.

"Max."

Max was another friend from school who she also reconnected with a few months ago. He was the medical examiner in town and had helped on a few cases.

"What happened with Elias?"

"We have been texting, but he never asked me out. Max did and I said yes."

"What does that mean for you and Elias?"

"I don't know. Maybe he'll find out about Max and get jealous." She chuckled. "I'm going to get ready. Sorry I'll miss seeing Kyle tonight."

"Officer Kyle is coming?" Ivy asked.

"Raff! Yay!" Dove cheered.

The girls loved it when Kyle Rafferty came over. He would play with them, tell them jokes, and give them quarters. For Christmas, they had each gotten a piggy bank and thanks to him, the banks were filling up quickly.

I was a bit nervous about him coming over tonight because I hoped to talk to him about Samir's murder. He wasn't going to be happy about me getting involved. I know Detective Upton had already talked to him about our relationship. Raff had relayed the conversation to me.

"Upton talked to me today," he had said.

"Uh-oh, this sounds bad. Is it bad?"

"Meh, not really. He just wanted to ensure our relationship, and any police cases, don't cross."

"What?"

"Yeah. I can't pass you information and you can't use me to get information." He winked.

"Darn, that's the only reason you're here." I laughed, squeezing his hand.

And that was it, we had agreed not to discuss cases, but now I really needed to do this for Fatima. She was the sweetest lady and deserved to have answers. What if she was in danger? Or worse, her children. Anwar might be a jerk, but I didn't wish him ill.

I didn't know Mona and Ayman well, but they all seemed sweet like Fatima. Anwar was the only thorn that I saw in their family.

The door opened and Shayla came in.

"Look who I found outside," she said coming in. Kyle Rafferty stepped in behind her.

"Officer Kyle!" the twins yelled and ran to him. He lifted them up into his arms.

"My favorite girls," he said, bouncing them around. "Hey, Jess."

"Hey, Raff." I smiled, then turned to Shayla. "Hey, Shay, how was work?"

"Not bad. Busy. We have a wedding coming up. They want things for various parties leading up to the big day. Cupcakes, cookies, various pastries. They asked for my eclairs."

"Nice. That sounds promising."

"You're famous," Ivy said.

"I want cookies," Dove said.

"Me too," Raff said.

"I brought some." Shayla held up a bag.

The three cheered while Shayla and I chuckled at their excitement.

She set the cookies on the counter. "For after dinner. I'm going to change."

"We're coming with you!" the girls said as Kyle set them down.

The sisters went upstairs. It gave me an opportunity to talk to Kyle without anyone hearing, but I was suddenly nervous. It had to be now, as I didn't know if I would get another chance.

"So, what's on the menu tonight?" he asked, coming to put his arms around me.

We had a very easy relationship. The affection felt natural.

"The girls' favorite. I don't have a good name for it, we just call it creamy, cheesy beefy pasta."

"Oh, I like that. I think we had that the first night I ate over."

"Yeah, probably. We have it all the time."

"Can I help?" He chuckled.

"Are you teasing me?" I laughed. I had a hard time sharing the kitchen with anyone except Shayla, but with her, our friendship started with the kitchen.

"Yeah. A little." He kissed me. "I'll just sit over here and keep you company."

"Perfect." I started pulling out ingredients. "Oh, by the way, I talked to Fatima Saad today."

"Jess, you know we can't talk about this."

"I know. I get it, but can I just ask one question?"

He sighed, dropping his head into his hands, then looked up. "Fine. One question, but that's it."

"Great." I steadied myself, because it was a big question. "She mentioned that the killer was waiting for Samir and was sitting in a chair, then they talked and argued before the person shot him."

"Um, yes, so what's your question?"

"Why is the media reporting it as a robbery?"

"That's a big question and not just a simple answer."

We heard the girls as they started to come back downstairs.

"Can we table it for now?" I asked.

"Yes, we'll need to."

"But you'll answer?"

"Yes." He smiled.

The girls came running towards him, jumping at him and laughing when he caught them midair.

"Come play in our room!"

"Yes, we can play with our dollhouse!"

They went to play while Shayla and I got to work on dinner. Vee came down dressed and ready for her date.

"Wow, you look gorgeous!" I said, hugging her.

"Thanks. Check my hair." She pointed at her perfectly styled hair. No frizz. It was beautiful.

"I know. You've been listening to me."

There was a knock at the door. Ivy and Dove came running.

"Can we open it?" they asked.

"Not this time," Vee said, as she opened it. "Hey, Max."

"Hey, Vee. Look at you. Wow." He stepped forward to kiss her cheek. He said hi to everyone, then they left.

Our dinner was ready, so we ate, then we played a board game with the girls. Shayla got them ready for bed, then said good night herself. It was finally down to just me and Rafferty again.

We were sitting in the living room watching television. I didn't want to push him to answer my somewhat loaded question. I knew it was not an easy one.

If he didn't tell me tonight, I would wait to ask him again. I didn't want to push my luck too much.

"So, you asked me a question earlier. Are you ready for the answer?"

I turned to face him. "Yes."

"Okay, I'm doing this because it's you. I could get in trouble. You understand that right?"

"I do and I won't say a word. Obviously, I don't want you in trouble."

"But you still want me to tell you." He chuckled softly as he pulled me in for a kiss.

When it ended, I mumbled yes.

He took a deep breath. "Robbery is what we have told the media for now and that we are doing further investigation, so not a complete lie. We just don't need them to report on the organized crime ring that we truly think is behind this."

"Organized crime," I repeated. That's what Fatima had said, too. It must be true then.

"Yes."

"How does that work?"

"That's a new question."

"But it isn't. It's about how this organized crime works. I ask because he has a restaurant and while I know cash is accepted, it isn't exactly a cash business. Isn't organized crime about laundering money and usually funneling it through cash businesses, like strip clubs, washaterias, and things like that?"

"You watch too much TV." He chuckled. "Yes, it can be that, but it's evolving too. So, in this case, they are investing in real estate or financing businesses, various ones. Though primarily focused on restaurants, there is a high failure rate which is good for these companies. They can then collect exorbitant fees on back loans and then take any collateral that was put up to secure the funds."

"Whoa." I didn't know what else to say. Though I knew a lot of failed restaurants.

"There are several parts to it. On one side, they fraudulently take money by making a lot of promises to investors. Then on the other, they loan money with complicated and intricate terms. So complex, in fact, it is sometimes difficult to know who the one is laundering the money and who the victims are. There will be legit companies getting money in legitimate ways layered in with a couple of these shell companies, and owned by non-existent companies or existing companies, like I said, legitimate companies."

My head was spinning. I could barely follow what he was saying. I simply nodded, so he continued.

"We have a small task force, and when I say small it is one person, who is working undercover. They are trying to learn the structure, but I can't say much. I'm not always in those debriefs with them. Some but not all. However, what I do know about this is confidential."

"I understand."

"Just know, we haven't turned a blind eye but have been working this for a few years."

"Years?"

"Yeah, and I think you'd be surprised who uses them and who doesn't." He sat back.

I just sat there stunned. Who used them? I didn't. Were they people I knew? People I was friends with? Why would they use a loan shark? Wait, was it a loan shark? That's just what I was picturing.

I guess not everyone had enough capital to invest in a business the way I had. It was just luck, and a little skill, that I won all those competitions and had been able to save so much.

Studying his profile, I wanted to know, to ask him more but did I really want to look under that rock? But then, if I didn't find out, I would always be looking sideways at my fellow chefs and restaurant owners.

I decided for tonight to just sit back and enjoy some cuddle time with my favorite cop. Tomorrow I would worry about finding Samir's killer and whatever I could about this organized crime.

Chapter Five

After Rafferty had left last night, I laid awake thinking about what he'd said. I knew there were different ways to launder money, and watching true crime shows like *American Greed* and heck, even the world news, I'd seen a lot of crazy investment schemes.

But I never thought there was stuff like that happening in Dashwood. We were small-town. Well, we might be a few people over small-town, but I'd been to big cities, we were so far removed from that.

People still waved to neighbors, helped each other, and looked out for each other. We had various festivals, parades, and farmers markets.

We knew each other, though it had gotten a lot larger since I was a child, and I didn't know as many people as I used to. After traveling and working briefly in other cities, coming home felt strange and foreign, yet oddly familiar, too. I guess some days it still did.

The realization that I didn't know this place quite like I think I did had those feelings of strangeness and unfamiliarity bubbling up again. But I was going to find out all I could, I just had to come up with a plan.

As I dressed for the day, I thought about what I needed to do. Research the leasing company that Samir and Anwar used for their business, knowing it would likely be a shell company or something to cover up the real investor, but it was a start.

Research would have to wait until later though. It was time for work.

I headed over early taking the long way so I could drive past the Spicy Fig Bistro. I pulled to the curb across the street looking at it. It was just plain and ordinary from the outside with the beige stucco exterior and plate-glass window. It was in a strip center with a nail salon on one side and a thrift shop on the other. All the businesses had the same generic sign with their shop name on it.

Fatima had told me they had no plans to open again soon. That made me a little sad. Samir was so proud of his restaurant and his food. He wanted to share it with everyone.

One time when I picked up a take-out order we talked about it.

"When I left Lebanon, I had a dream to share my food with people. Food was so important to me and my family growing up. All my favorite memories are tied to eating my mother's hummus or falafels with tzatziki. She also made a beautiful lamb shank or her shawarma. I miss her food so much." He smiled sadly but then continued.

"When I first moved to the United States, I was only eighteen. I took odd jobs in kitchens and saved my money. It took me fifteen years to get my first restaurant, but I did it. Unfortunately, that one burned down. The insurance didn't cover the cost to reopen so I took a job doing taxes. It was another six years and a move to another state, but I finally saved enough to open my second restaurant."

"Where was that one?"

"Florida. Orlando area."

"And what happened with that one?"

"There were so many other restaurants, we just didn't get enough business and had to close. Then I took a job in Texas, over in Pinehurst. That's how we ended up here, but it took time and an investor to get enough to open this place."

"Well, perhaps, third time's a charm?"

"Here's hoping." He handed me the bag of food. "Enjoy and see you next time."

Now as I drove away from the closed Spicy Fig, I thought of him saying it took an investor. Had he known what that investor was doing? That it was basically an organized crime ring charging crazy fees and interest on the loans?

I also wondered how many of these other restaurants had investors. Did they understand the consequences of their loan or whatever the arrangements were?

I pulled into the back parking lot of The Crock Pot and a slow smile spread across my face. This was something I had done all by myself. My hard work and years of saving had gotten me here.

I loved my place. It was a standalone building with a large front parking lot and a small back lot. It was perfect to separate customers from employees.

I took in the red-white brick exterior and the blue awnings that shaded the large windows that ran along all sides of the dining room, giving good views of the street. The ornate wooden front double doors sat at an angle. There was a sign with the words *The Crock Pot* over the door in a font that Vee had created especially for me. She was a wonderful artist but rarely showcased it.

I headed in, punching in the code. The lights came on in my beautiful kitchen. It still took my breath away a little bit.

It made me sad that there were chefs in town being taken advantage of, but proud that I hadn't had to go to such extremes.

After resetting the alarm, I headed to the office, dropped my stuff into my desk, then fired up the computers and printer. Next, I wrote Tomato Basil on our white board that announced the soup of the day to the staff, then I headed to the kitchen to start getting the prep going for the day.

Hours later, we were on the other side of the lunch rush and were cleaning up, prepping for the rest of the day. That's when my phone rang. It was Shayla.

"Hey, Shay, what's up?"

"The girls got in some fight with another kid at school. I have to go meet with them, but I'm nervous to go alone, can you meet me there?"

"Of course!" I looked around. Eli was the only one here. I could message June to see if she could come in early. "I'll meet you there." I hung up and turned to Eli. "Do you think you can manage the kitchen until June comes in?"

"Yes, I can, Chef."

"I have a family situation that I need to take care of."

"Not a problem. I can do it."

I didn't have much choice. I nodded and left to wash up before heading to the office.

"There's a problem with the little girls. I have to go," I told Noah. "Can you ask June to come in a bit earlier, if she can?"

"Absolutely. And if she can't?"

I stood there holding my purse, contemplating my options. "Hope that Eli has had enough training to keep up and manage the kitchen."

He nodded. "No worries, Chef. We will manage this. Take care of the girls."

I stopped by to check on Eli on the way out.

"I promise, Chef, I got this." He smiled. "Go, go. We'll be fine."

I nodded and had to trust my staff. I had more important things to worry about. Calmly, or as calmly as possible, I drove across town to the elementary school.

Pulling in, I saw Shayla getting out of her car. She looked over as I parked next to her.

"Hey. Thanks so much for coming," she said as I climbed out of my car.

"Of course. What do you know?"

"A little girl was teasing them, and they had enough, but there are two of them and one of her." She frowned.

"Okay, let's go see what the punishment is."

"I hate that they are only eight and already having trouble with school."

"Even though they both seem so well adjusted to things, doesn't mean they are and perhaps we should look into that therapy that the child services people were recommending."

"You're probably right," she said as she swung the door open to the elementary school. "I have been looking at them, just need to pick one."

As we stepped in, I was hit with a wave of nostalgia. It happened each time I stepped through the doors. I would flash back to being a small child on my way to kindergarten, walking through the same doors. The smell of old books, fresh crayons, and pencil shavings.

I remember holding my father's hand as he walked me to the first day of class. It was back when things were normal, before everything changed.

Nothing about the building had changed much though. It still had the same dingy vinyl floors, pasty looking cinder block walls, children's artwork plastered all over it.

We turned left into the office. Ivy and Dove were sitting in chairs behind the reception desk. Their eyes were red and puffy. They looked up as we came in which started another crying round.

"I'm so sorry. I didn't mean to," Dove whispered.

"Me too," Ivy said, clinging to her sister's hand.

"It's okay. We'll figure this out," Shayla said. "Hi, we're here to meet with Mrs. Kane and Ms. Flowers."

"Yes, of course. I'll let them know." She walked down a short hall. We could hear the voices, then she stuck her head out, gesturing to us. "Ladies?"

Shayla smiled at the girls, and I mouthed that we'd be right back. We followed her to a conference room at the end of the hallway. Mrs. Kane and Ms. Flowers were waiting for us there.

I had only met Mrs. Kane once but I knew Ms. Gloria Flowers because we had gone to school together, at least until I transferred to the culinary arts school.

It was a little strange to see my former classmate working at the school we had gone to once upon a time. I still remember jumping rope with her.

She nodded at me as we all took seats.

"Thank you for coming, Ms. Boyd and Ms. Vasquez," Mrs. Kane started. "As we mentioned on the phone, Ivy and Dove had an issue on the playground today with another little girl."

"Can we know the details of what led up to it? I mean, what specifically was said to start the fight," I asked?

I only knew the girls closely for about a month, but I had known them longer than that. Yes, they had gone through a lot. Despite all of it, they still had some of the innocence and joy that only young kids could have.

So, this seemed out of character for them both.

"Well, the other little girl has been teasing Ivy and Dove about losing their mother, about their father being in jail, and now about their grandmother. Today they just had enough, and Dove hit her first, then when the little girl hit Dove, Ivy stepped in. We know that she has been bullying them and are taking appropriate actions to also punish her," Ms. Flowers said.

"Okay. Then this seems fairly cut and dry," I said, then looked at Shayla. She simply nodded. Her stony expression told me she was shutdown. "What punishment will Ivy and Dove get?"

The principal and assistant principal looked at each other. Then, Mrs. Kane said, "we thought a one-day suspension would be appropriate."

"A suspension?" Shayla blurted out as she sat forward. "They were being bullied and fought back."

I set a hand on one of Shayla's. She sat back.

"We understand and believe me when I say the other girl is getting a longer suspension, but we can't have fighting in the school either," Mrs. Kane said.

"I was them as a kid. Mrs. Kane, you were here. You should remember that," Shayla said. Mrs. Kane nodded and started to speak, but Shayla continued. "Nothing was done to those kids, but I was sent home time and time again. I know you said the other girl is also being punished, but I want to ensure that Ivy and Dove are not the only ones being punished here. They are good girls who have had a rough life at only eight years old. Their father and grandmother are in prison for life. Our mother is dead. Our only other relative doesn't want us, so it is on me to raise them! I'm only eighteen!"

She burst into tears, sobbing into her hands. I rarely see her cry, but sometimes when the strong break, they break hard. I should know.

"Shayla, I do remember and I'm sorry for that. We have since changed our policies significantly. We have a no tolerance for bullies or fighting of any kind. All parties involved in the fight are punished, not just those who started it."

Shayla calmed down a little. "I won't punish the girls further, but we accept the suspension."

"Okay."

"Is there any work or anything we can have them do while they are out?" I asked.

"I will ask their teacher," Ms. Flowers said. "Be right back."

"Do you have any other questions?"

"I don't. Shayla?" I looked at her.

"No, nothing."

"Okay, why don't I walk you out and you can wait with the girls while Ms. Flowers confirms with their teacher about homework."

We walked back to the reception area. The twins sat up straighter as tears started to fall, but they didn't make a sound. Shayla picked up Ivy, then sat with her in her lap, then pulled Dove to her. The sisters sat comforting each other, tears falling.

I knew they all needed to see a therapist, and I would make sure it happened. Auntie Rita had insisted that I talk to someone years ago, and I think it had helped at least process the trauma. Life still wasn't perfect growing up with an absent mother and a father in prison, but whose life was perfect.

Minutes later, Ms. Flowers returned with a stack of worksheets.

"Mrs. Richards also wants to remind them to do their twenty minutes of reading."

"Okay, thanks, Gloria ... Oh, I mean Ms. Flowers," I said taking the sheets.

"Ha, Jess, you're an adult. Only the kids have to call me Ms. Flowers."

"Yeah, it seems weird to call you that."

"Remember your fifth birthday party?" Gloria asked.

"I do."

"That was the best birthday party I had been to."

I smiled and we said goodbye. The three girls walked quietly to the car.

"Are we in big trouble?" Ivy asked as I helped buckle her into the car.

"Only a little trouble," I said.

"And only with the school. You'll have to stay home tomorrow," Shayla said.

"Yay! No school," they cheered.

"No, it's punishment for getting in a fight," Shayla said. "It isn't a fun day. Mrs. Richards sent work."

"Boo."

"Not fair."

We shut the doors.

"You okay?" I asked Shayla.

"Yes. No. I can't stay home with them tomorrow."

"I'm off so I'll watch them."

"Seriously?"

"Yeah, I had nothing planned."

"Ohmygosh, you're the best!" She launched herself into my arms, hugging me tight. "I can always count on you."

I wanted to reply but the lump in my throat didn't allow it. I'd cry those happy tears on the way home while I followed them in my car.

Except for giving me an opportunity to fall apart, I wish we were travelling in the same car, so I could talk to the three sisters. Their mental health was fragile right now and I wanted to comfort them. Coming from a traumatic childhood myself, I could relate.

When we got home, I helped her get the girls out of the car. All three had red eyes and the younger two were sniffling. Clearly it was a tearful ride home.

Ivy and Dove shuffled inside, heads hung and went straight to their rooms. There were sounds of crying. Lulu appeared and joined them.

At least she would be a comfort, I thought as I put their backpacks in the front closet, then turned to Shayla.

"You okay?"

"I'm just so worried about them. One minute they seem fine and the next they are crying, and now this. Fighting at school." She exhaled heavily, her shoulders dropping. "I don't want them going down the path I took."

"You turned out okay," I said softly.

"Ha, barely. If it wasn't for you, I may not have gotten this far."

"You know that's not true right?" She shrugged in reply, so I continued. "No, it's true. You were on the fast track to graduation long before I met you. You were excelling in all your classwork and you more than stood out in Mr. Jones's class. I noticed you that first day I went to recruit apprentices for The Crock Pot."

"You did?"

"Yes, you were clearly something special. You had leadership skills and talent in the kitchen. I watched as the other students looked to you for direction."

She straightened her back. "I guess you're right."

"And with the right guidance, your sisters will overcome this too."

"Thanks. I hope so. It's a lot of pressure." She smiled weakly. "But it is worth it to have them here with me."

"Now tell me what their punishment is."

She looked towards their room. "I really didn't say much to them actually. They are just hurt, lost, and know that fighting is wrong."

"Why are they in their room then?"

"They did that. I really don't want to punish them at all. Yes, I want them to do their schoolwork, but otherwise, I see this as a mental health day for them."

"Plus, tomorrow is Friday, so they will have the weekend to relax," I said.

"Very true." She looked at me. "I better go check on them."

I nodded then went upstairs to change. When I came back, the girls were still in the twins' room, so I started preparing our dinner.

Twenty minutes later, the sisters came out laughing. From there the evening went as normal.

Chapter Six

The girls watched a movie in the morning while I cleaned the house a bit. I brought them some popcorn about halfway through, taking a seat between them to watch the last half. They smiled at me, then each leaned against me.

As someone who never thought she'd have kids, it was a strange place to be now. I had taken in a teenager when she had nowhere else to go. Now her little sisters. I enjoyed every minute of it though.

When the movie finished, I got the girls settled in with their schoolwork. While they worked on it, I pulled out my laptop to research the leasing company.

I typed in the company's web address and the screen populated. The home screen was a gallery of properties they manage. I noticed a few I recognized. In addition to the strip center that Spicy Fig Bistro was in, I saw that Beaks and Brews and Pins Bowling Alley were also under their management.

I wouldn't have thought Nathan would make such a shady deal. Did he know what this leasing company was about? We'd been friends for a long time, and I thought he was smarter than that.

Not that Samir was dumb for signing up, though I suppose it was actually Anwar who made the final deal. People got scammed every day, so that could be the case with Nathan and the Saads.

I looked through the site. They had bios of their staff from the VP to the leasing agents. The one for Dashwood was Penny Galindo.

I hit the contact me button, jotting down the phone number. I couldn't call while the girls were in earshot because I couldn't risk them overhearing then telling people my fake plans.

The idea was I would make an appointment to discuss a lease with them and possibly see available properties so I could open a new restaurant. This way I could hear what type of pitch they make to prospective customers.

To further the illusion that this was real, I would say that with The Crock Pot, I needed extra capital. I hoped it was believable.

"Jess, I'm ready for my reading."

"Me too," Dove added.

"Okay. Ivy first and then you." I closed my laptop and went to sit with Ivy so she could read to me. Dove sat nearby listening and holding her book. When she was done, we listened to Dove read.

"Homework done?"

"Yes."

"Mine is."

"Do y'all want to go to the park?" It was a little cool out, but the sun was shining, and it wasn't raining so I thought we should take advantage of the good weather. It would wear them out.

"The hiking one or the playground one?" Dove asked.

"Which one do you want to go to?"

They looked at each other, then yelled their answer in unison.

"Hiking one!"

"Sounds good. Go put on your shoes, grab your jackets, go potty, and then meet me back here. Okay?"

"Okay!" they yelled and scrambled away to do what I asked. I got my jacket, shoes, and a few bottles of water.

I loved that they wanted to go to Milton County Park to hike. While most children might have wanted to go to a playground, they had picked my most favorite place.

I loved spending my free time along the nature trails walking around the lake, listening to the birds and watching squirrels scurry around. It was the best self-care that I knew of. I hoped it helped them as well.

The girls came running from the bathroom with jackets and shoes on.

"Ready!"

"Me too."

"Alrighty, let's roll."

They scrambled into the car, then sang all the way to the park, cheering when I pulled into the parking lot. I smiled at them in the rearview mirror.

Once the car was stopped, they hopped out and ran to the sign with the trail map on it.

"Which trail do you want to take?" I asked.

"I want to go this way. There are always ducks by the water!" Dove said.

"Yeah, ducks trail."

"Alrighty, ducks trail it is."

This trail was roughly two miles, and my favorite one. Not only because it had views of the ducks, but at about the halfway point there was a beautiful wooden pier and observation deck. It had the best views of the lake from there.

The other trail was two and a half miles but didn't have the same lake view until nearly the end when it met up with this trail right after the observation deck. It was a good one for seeing deer and rabbits, but not much else.

The girls skipped along, singing and holding hands. As much as they wanted to see animals on this walk, I knew they wouldn't making that much noise, but I let them enjoy themselves.

I focused on them and tried to keep my mind off of Chef Nathan and if he could be wrapped up with the same company that the Saads were. It didn't work of course; my mind went right to it. I wish we still had the murder board, but with the girls moving in, we had stopped using it.

Maybe I could find a new place for it. Somewhere they wouldn't see it. I'd have to think about the case and study the clues. I'm not completely sure if it had helped with my past cases, but it didn't hurt.

Dove skipped over to hold my hand.

"I don't see any squirrels today," she said.

"I think you both are being a little loud for them."

"Oh." She looked around. "Ivy, we need to be quiet, so the squirrels come out!"

"Then don't yell!" Ivy yelled back.

"I'm not!"

"Yes you are!"

"Okay, okay. Let's all quiet down," I said, trying not to laugh.

Once they finally did quiet down, they got their wish of seeing the different animals.

We saw bluejays, cardinals, and small finch. They would fly from tree to tree, chirping and singing. Then along the shore, turtles popped their heads up and a few ducks swam around.

A fat little squirrel ran out onto the trail, looked at us, twitching its little nose, before running back into the woods. The girls looked at me with pure joy in their faces at the interaction.

We arrived at my favorite part where a wooden pier goes out over the water.

We walked out on the dock taking in the view of the entire lake. Along the shoreline not far from us, we saw a large heron fishing.

"Look, Jess." Dove pointed, trying to whisper. The heron didn't even look up. "It isn't scared."

"Oh, it got a fish." Ivy giggled.

The heron swallowed it down then flew across the lake. They oohed and awed as it took flight. The wingspan was impressive. We stood there for several minutes just taking it in.

"Mama would have loved this," Ivy said.

"She would have."

"Did she ever bring you here?"

"No, but Shayla did."

"Yeah, Shayla did. She would take mama's car or have a friend give us a ride."

"We would get to run and be loud, like we couldn't at home."

"Yeah."

Now I understood why they wanted to come and why they had been running and yelling when we first arrived. I felt a bit bad for making them stop. If they got loud again, I would just let them.

"How are you feeling now?" I asked them.

"What do you mean?" Dove asked.

"Hungry," Ivy said.

"Okay, hungry. We can go eat as soon as we leave, but Dove, what I mean is, are you sad, happy, angry, whatever?"

Dove screwed up her face as she tapped a finger against her lips.

"I'm angry at Grandma Lynn for leaving us and angry at Daddy for killing our mother, but I'm also angry at mama for not doing better," she finally said, then started weeping quietly. "We're just little girls. We need a mother."

Wow, that was articulate for an eight-year-old. Perhaps I underestimated them and their processing of this situation. I did have a feeling some of this was stuff that Shayla had talked to them about.

Ivy made a slight sound as she began crying too, then wrapped her arms around her sister.

I watched the two sisters for a moment. A ping of jealousy went through me, not because I was envious of two hurt, lost little girls. When my life imploded, I didn't have a sibling to go through that with. They had each other and big sister, Shayla.

Then I thought of Anwar, Mona, and Ayman. They could mourn their father together. Though Anwar didn't seem close to his younger siblings. However, I didn't know them all that well, so maybe they were closer than they appeared.

Like me, Anwar was much older than his younger two siblings. He was my age while Mona was in her mid-twenties and Ayman was Shayla's age.

"I'm so sorry, girls." I pulled them into my arms as I sat on a nearby bench. "At least you have each other and Shayla to lean on, right?"

"And you." Ivy sniffed.

"And Auntie Vee," Dove added with a slight smile.

"And Raff!" Ivy said with a little giggle.

"And Granny Ines."

"And Auntie Rita."

"And ... oh, Sawyer and Riley!" Dove clapped.

"We have a lot of people," Ivy said.

"You do. You really do, and I know it hurts to not have your mother. She loved you both very much."

They nodded. Shayla was still trying to wade through all the medical insurance and survivor benefits for her sisters, but as soon as it was figured out, she was getting them in with a good therapist. Until then, this was all I could do.

"Now, where should we go for ice cream?" I asked.

"We scream!" they yelled. It was the best ice cream in Dashwood.

"And can we go to Mr. Monte's comic book shop first?" Dove asked. She was a budding artist and loved to go look at all the great artwork on the wall. Ivy wasn't as into that but did like looking at all the superhero figures and pop figurines like Vee.

"Well, let's go!"

We walked back to the trail so we could start making our way back to the parking lot. I didn't fuss this time as they stomped, sang, and laughed. It was a beautiful day. Plus, the trees and flowers couldn't run from the noise, so I just looked at that as we finished the last half of our hike.

We still had about half a mile left when I noticed a man walking towards us. He seemed out of place somehow, but I couldn't put my finger on why. He was dressed in joggers and a black T-shirt. Nothing weird about that, but there was just something about him.

"Hi, good afternoon," he said as he got close.

"Good afternoon," I said.

The girls, thankfully, just waved but kept skipping and laughing along.

He passed us with only that greeting and a nod. I didn't turn to watch him, at first. I didn't want to seem obvious. Instead, I stopped like I needed to tie my shoe. It gave me the opportunity to look around without seeming too suspicious, at least I hoped.

He never looked back. Simply kept on walking. I shook off my paranoid thoughts and continued following the twins.

So, silly, I chastised myself.

When they spotted the car, they raced each other there. I think they made it at the same time but spent most of the car ride across town arguing about who won. They tried pulling me into it, but when I suggested a tie, they didn't like that.

"Someone has to win," Ivy argued.

"Yeah, then how do you know who the loser is?"

"Wait? Nobody has to be a loser. Did you have fun?"

"Yes," they both said.

"Then you are both winners, right?" I peeked at them in the rearview mirror. I saw them exchange a look, then burst into laughter.

"We both won!" They cheered.

Glad that was settled, I thought as I pulled into the parking lot between Heroes and Villains Comic, Roasted Beans Coffee, and We Scream Ice Cream Parlor.

There was a small garden at the far end of the parking lot then there was a second shopping area much like this one with Nearly New Thrift store and Polly's Pizzeria. Across the street was another strip center with the tattoo shop and a dentist's office.

Monte greeted the girls and then they ran around looking at this and that. I bought them each one thing. Dove got a small print of the lake. It was by local artist Susan Dane. She signed all her prints with Suzy D. They were always landscapes from other Dashwood or surrounding areas.

"I love this Ms. Suzy D. She always paints what she sees," Dove said with a huge grin.

I couldn't argue with that. I had a few Suzy D's hanging in the restaurant.

Ivy then picked out a superhero.

"He'll protect us," she said with a nod.

"I feel safer already."

Monte added a few stickers for them and then we headed over to the ice cream shop. We walked in and the two people behind the counter yelled, "We scream for ice cream!"

The girls let out a giggle and ran to peek into the displays.

"Hey, Jess!" the owner, Zelda greeted. "I haven't seen you in a few weeks. How's it going?"

"Good. How are things?" I asked.

"A little slow with winter but starting to pick up now that we have a few warmer days."

"Oh, who is your leasing company here?" I already knew the answer, but I pretended I didn't.

I knew the company didn't own all these businesses, like Monte's or the tattoo shop which had been in the area since before I was born. They were independently owned, but some of the newer places were not.

Her face paled a bit and had I not been looking right at her, I wouldn't have noticed the change. She composed herself quickly. "Um, why? You looking at a change?"

"No, well, maybe. Thinking of opening a second business and just doing research."

"I, um, don't recommend these people." She looked over her shoulder. The two employees were busy with the girls, giving out samples and telling them jokes. "They have strict terms and ... well, you'd be better off doing things yourself."

"What do you mean?"

"I really can't talk about it. But all I will say is if I would have known before, what I know now, I would have done anything else but get into business with them." She tapped the counter, then went to join the employees and the girls.

I really want to push her, but her tense body and whispered words had me looking around. Were they here? Were they listening? Is that what had gotten Samir in trouble?

The girls got a single scoop in a sugar cone, and I got a small milkshake, then we went to sit outside. Zelda followed us with a bottle of water.

She lifted the bottle to her lips, but before she drank whispered. "I'm happy to talk with you at your restaurant sometime."

"Okay, I'm there mostly in the day, but happy to meet anytime."

She nodded. "How are those cones, girls?" she asked loudly.

"So good."

"The best!"

She sat with us until the girls were nearly finished, just chatting about the weather or the upcoming art festival.

"I heard you are going to have a food booth this time," she said.

"I am. Serving gumbo as a nod to my grandfather," I shared. "He loved gumbo, and it was one of the few things I ever saw him cook himself."

"Oh, that's nice. Your alphabet soup was inspired by your grandmother, wasn't it?"

"Yes, it was."

"Nice. Well, my break is over. I'm glad you ladies stopped by today. Have a wonderful day." She smiled, then nodded at me as if in secret code. "I'll see you again soon."

"She's so nice," Dove said, as she ate her last bite.

"She is." Ivy grinned.

Chapter Seven

When we got home, the girls ran straight to their room with their new possessions. Dove with her new print and Ivy with her figurine.

"I'm going to find a place for my new picture!" Dove announced.

They had the room with the old murder board in it, which was really just an oversized corkboard. She could put a push pin in it and hang the framed print easily without help. They already had other pictures and posters hung that way.

"I'm going to take my superhero to our dollhouse. He'll be the security guard," Ivy said, running off.

I wanted to ask her about the security guard, but decided it was best not to know.

Sawyer and Riley had gotten them a huge dollhouse for Christmas with all the furniture, more furniture and accessories than they could possibly use in that one dollhouse. They would spend hours decorating and redecorating, then playing house with their dolls.

While they were occupied, I called the leasing company and spoke with a scheduler. He made me an appointment to meet with Penny Galindo for next week.

"Okay, that's done," I said to myself.

Then I just sat there wishing I had the murder board to add the appointment to. Plus, I would add that weird conversation with Zelda.

I wish she would have been able to say more.

"Honey, I'm home!" Vee yelled as she burst through the door.

It reminded me of when Sawyer lived here with us. That was his daily greeting. I'm glad to hear that Vee was keeping it alive.

Ivy and Dove came running from their room.

"Auntie Vee!"

"Hey." She hugged them. "Did you have a good day?"

They both started telling her all about our day. She seemed to understand them, even though they started in different places in the day and talked over each other. Then when they tried to drag her into their room to play, she asked if she could have a minute to change.

"Yes! You can meet Steve the security guard," Ivy said.

"We'll go wait for you."

"Okay, but it might be longer than a minute."

"That's okay. We understand grown up minutes," Ivy said, running off, Dove right behind her.

"Oh, my. They're sassy." Vee laughed. "I love having them here, but um, who is Steve?"

"The security guard."

"I guess I'll have to go find out." She laughed.

"So, how was work?"

"Oh, you know, work."

"You aren't letting people yell at you for things that aren't your fault again, are you?"

People took out their postal frustrations on my poor friend. Her main job was to sell stamps and take packages. She wasn't the one doing the delivery.

"Of course not. They're just venting."

"Um, I don't like that, Vee. You are too nice."

"I have to be, but it doesn't bother me. Rolls off my back." She laughed. "So, tell me about your day. How were the girls, really?"

"So much fun, but I think once Shayla has all their medical stuff sorted out, therapy will help them a lot."

"I'm sure."

"Oh," I lowered my voice. "I made myself an appointment with that leasing company."

"Oh, when? Do you need me to go with you?" Vee asked.

"I don't think so, but it's on Wednesday. Also, I talked to Zelda."

"What did she say?"

"Not much but just acted suspicious. Said she would have to talk to me somewhere else."

"Juicy! I wish we still had the murder board."

"I keep thinking that too."

"What if we put it … um … where aren't the girls allowed?" She thought, scanning the first floor. "Do they go in your closet?"

"No, they don't and it's large enough we could make something in there."

"We could use poster board and sticky notes."

"I don't have any poster board."

"Oh, I have a large cardboard box that we could use for now," Vee offered.

"Okay, we'll do it once the girls go to bed," I said.

"It's a plan. Well, I better hurry up and change so I can meet Steve the security guard."

Later after the girls were in bed, we filled Shayla in on what we were doing.

"Oh, I have some poster board left over from when I was in school. We had a lot of projects," she said.

"Really? That's great. All I had was an old box," Vee said.

"I'll grab the sticky notes and a couple of markers, then we can meet in my room," I said.

Vee went to her room to grab a chair while Shayla and I gathered the supplies. Back in my room, we laid the poster board out on the bed, then Shayla climbed onto my bed. I stood over it.

"Okay, what do we know at this point?" I said, marker uncapped and ready to write.

"Well, victim is obvious," Vee said.

"Yes." I wrote Samir. "And Fatima shared he was part of some military group back in the 80s. That's why they moved to America."

"That was a long time ago, would that still be a threat?"

"No idea, but we can't rule it out since she thought it was important enough to mention."

"What about the security footage?" Shayla asked.

"Yes, that person looked very military-like." I had the marker poised. "But what do I write?"

"Can you just write shooter?" Shayla asked.

"Yes, with a question mark after," I said, writing it down.

"Then the leasing company," Vee added. I wrote it.

"I hate to say, but we need to write Anwar and his choices," I said, waiting to write that until they agreed.

"Yeah, I think you're right."

"And especially after Zelda was acting so weird. I hope I can meet with her soon."

"What do you think she'll say, if and when you do?"

"Well, I hope she tells me why she warned me from using that company and what kind of lease she has."

"Did Fatima give you any information about their lease?" Shayla asked.

"Not really. I got the idea that she didn't know about the business part of things."

"From what we've been hearing, Anwar handled a lot of the business and Samir mostly cooked and was the face of the place," Vee said.

"Where did you hear that?"

"Post office. People chat."

"They talk about that?"

"People talk about everything and everyone." Vee chuckled. "It's spicier than any beauty salon I've ever been to."

"Well, okay." I wrote Anwar - handles business.

I shuffled the clues around on the board, until they made sense to me. I then held it up to get a better look at it.

"Okay, what do we think so far?"

"I think it's a good start."

"I agree."

We looked at it for a few silent moments. My brain couldn't connect the clues yet, especially the 1980s military service. That one seemed out of left field, but Fatima thought it was important enough to mention now.

"It has to be this leasing company or someone associated with it, like that organized crime stuff that Raff was talking about, right?" I said.

"That's all I can think of."

"Yeah, has to be."

"Okay, well I guess I'll see what Zelda has to say, once I get to talk to her. Then I have that appointment with the leasing company next week."

"Movie?" Vee asked.

"Yes."

"Sounds good."

With that, I tucked the makeshift murder board in the back of my closet, facing the wall. I hoped it was out of sight enough to avoid any uncomfortable questions from the twins, though they were rarely in my room.

Chapter Eight

Zelda called while we were about to head out the door to Granny's for Sunday dinner. At least Sawyer was meeting us there. He would not be happy with anything that slowed us down. He was probably already there nibbling on any appetizer or snack that Granny would allow.

When my phone rang, I almost didn't answer because I didn't recognize the number.

"It's local, so …" I shrugged showing the phone to Vee.

"Yeah, answer it."

"Hello?"

"Hey, Jess? It's Zelda." Her voice trembled slightly.

"Oh, hey, Zelda. What's up?"

"Um, so sorry about the other day. I just couldn't talk at my place."

"That's okay. Come see me at mine."

"Great. Yes, that's what I wanted to ask. The shop is closed on Mondays, so I wanted to see if you're working."

"I am. I usually get there between eight and nine, then doors open at eleven to customers. If you want to meet before eleven, just let me know."

"Perfect. I'll come by early as long as I don't get in your way."

"Nah, we've got opening down to a science. I can spare ten or fifteen minutes for a friend. Just call my phone when you arrive, and I'll let you in."

"Okay, then I'll see you tomorrow morning. Take care."

"You too."

"She's coming to the restaurant?" Vee asked.

"Yep."

"I hope she's got some good info for you."

"Me too."

The girls came running at that moment. Thank goodness they hadn't overheard my conversation. Not that I had said anything about a murder, but they always asked a million questions. Sometimes I'd get tripped up, then say too much which led to a million more questions.

"Ready." Ivy giggled.

"Me too." her twin chimed in.

A frazzled Shayla followed behind them. She simply nodded.

We hopped in my car. Vee sat in the back with the twins. On the way over, the little girls chatted about everything and nothing. Somehow Vee always seemed to keep up with the conversation without trouble. It was amazing.

"Is Rafferty going to make it today?" Shayla asked me quietly. She likely didn't want the girls to overhear in case he didn't make it.

"Yeah, he's going to meet us there. He said he would be a touch late."

"Good. The girls will enjoy seeing him and Sawyer."

"Yeah, they are both great guys."

"I want them to see some positive males so hopefully they don't make the same mistake mom did."

I turned my head to glance at her. "Is that something you are worried about for yourself, too?"

She hadn't dated as far as I could tell. Never even seemed interested in guys, so I thought perhaps she was queer. But no, it seemed she had other concerns and likely needed therapy as much as the little girls.

"Yes, I'm very worried about that. I was watching a video. It was a clip of a talk show. The host, or doctor, whatever he is, said that you end up with someone like your own father. I have never really had a father, but the men in my life haven't been the greatest either. My father's dead, my first stepfather is in prison and then Mikey came out of prison to be my third stepfather." She looked over her shoulder. "They deserve better."

"I have said it before, but I am saying it again. So do you. You deserve wonderful things."

She smiled.

We pulled up at Granny and Auntie Rita's house to see a bunch of cars. I recognized Sawyer's and Kyle Rafferty's but the other one, I wasn't sure.

"Is that your mom's car?" Vee asked from the back seat.

Oh, bleep!

"It is." Dread spread through my body as I parked in front of the house.

The girls were excited to see everyone, but they hadn't met my mom, stepfather, or my brothers yet.

"Wait? Ivy. Dove," I said, waving them to me. "Okay, it looks like besides Raff, Sawyer, Riley, Granny and Auntie Rita, my mother, stepfather, and my brothers are here."

"You have brothers?" Ivy yelled.

"Um, yes, and they are here now," I whispered.

"Why are you telling us? Can't we just go in?" Dove asked, looking around.

"Yeah, I'm hungry," Ivy added.

"Yeah, let's go." I don't even know why I bothered to say anything.

It wasn't like I was going to tell them that I'm not a fan of my own mother. My stepfather's voice was like nails on a chalkboard. Then there were my brothers.

How could I even describe at an eight-year-old's level what was wrong with my relationship with my brothers? I didn't even understand it because it was mostly that I was jealous of them. Resented that they got the mother I used to have. The caring, loving mother who asked about your day, hugged you, and made you dinner.

I lost that mother when I was only five years old, and she never returned to me. I got a different mother years later.

Usually, Granny or Auntie Rita greeted us on the porch, so when they didn't, I wasn't sure what to do. The front door was open, so I opened the screen door and peeked inside.

I heard laughter from the kitchen.

"Hello," I called out.

"Back here!" someone yelled.

Another round of laughter. We followed the sound to find that Kyle had everyone mesmerized with his storytelling skills. He was a good storyteller.

Back in our school days, everyone would sit up and pay attention whenever Kyle got up to present a book report or present his project on the Civil War. Nobody else garnered that much attention.

I was surprised to see him as he thought he might be late, but I am so glad he made it. He would be a good distraction from my mother.

He saw me and a broad smile filled his face. Everyone turned.

"Raff!" Ivy yelled, running to him. He scooped her up.

"Hey, Ivy."

"Sawyer!" Dove yelled, running to him.

Sawyer was seated, so he pulled her into his lap. Riley was next to him. She leaned over to hug the little girl. The trio began a secret conversation.

Granny came to hug me. "You look well, mija."

"Thanks. I feel good."

"You see your mother's here," she whispered as she hugged me.

"I do."

"Not my idea. She called and I tried to say no, but here they are."

"It's okay."

I turned to my mom who had her back to me, and looked really engaged in a discussion with Christopher, the oldest of my two brothers.

"Hi, mom, good to see you," I said from behind her. She kept talking to Chris. He eyed me, then looked at her, then back to me before pointing at me.

"Oh, Jessie, I didn't see you there," Mom said over her shoulder. It was almost patronizing.

"Hey, Chris," I said, instead of playing her game.

"Hey, Messy-Jessie," he teased. "Your boyfriend is funny."

"Yeah, um, thanks." I looked over at Kyle who was now entertaining both young girls. "So, mom, it's good to see y'all here today. How are you?"

"Oh, just fine. Not that you call or ask otherwise. We had to come here to meet your boyfriend."

I wanted to say phones work both ways, but it wouldn't matter.

"Yeah, I'm sorry. Busy running my restaurant and helping with raising the girls."

"I don't know why you have to always take in strays," she said a little too loudly.

Everyone turned to look at her.

Ivy looked up at Rafferty. "What does she mean?"

"Nothing. Why don't we go outside and play tag?" he suggested to the girls.

"We'll come with you," Sawyer said. He and Riley, along with Vee and Shayla followed, them out into the backyard.

"Now, Margot, don't you start nothing," Samuel said, reaching for her hand. She pulled it back.

"What? I'm not starting anything. It was just a question for my daughter."

"Margot," Samuel warned. "You agreed to be nice."

"I *am* nice. She's the one who ruins everything."

"How am I ruining everything?" I looked around as if the answer would be in the room with us.

"You can't just have a normal life. Taking in children who aren't yours. You should be married with children of your own."

"She's a hero to those three girls, for caring for and loving them when they had nobody," Auntie Rita said. "They lost their mother, their home, everything. I think *you* of all people can understand that."

"Why me? My mother is still alive, and I have a beautiful home and family," Mom said with a shrug.

"You know why, Margot. Don't make me say it," Auntie Rita said.

"Say it. I dare you!" Mom stood and faced my aunt.

Auntie Rita straightened her back, standing taller. I could see the lifelong dancer in her stance with her tall, lean frame and long lines.

"You were a bad mother to Jessie. You failed her." Her voice so calm and smooth it sent a chill down my spine.

But I knew what was coming next. This was a fight that happened several times before. Bryan and Christopher exchanged a smirk, because they'd also heard it over and over.

"Yeah? Yeah? I may be a bad mother, but at least I *am* a mother."

"Ha, ha, ha. Yeah, well God didn't give me kids because he knew I'd have to help raise one of yours." She stepped closer to my mom. She towered over my short, petite mother.

"You think you're better than me because of your family's money, but you're no better."

"Oh, no, honey, I am so much better than you and your selfish attitude."

"Selfish? Me? Oh, sweetie, they don't even have a word for what you are."

"Generous? Loving? Giving? There are a lot of words for what I am and only one for you … but I can't say it in mixed company and on a Sunday!"

They stood there squared off as if they were going to brawl at any moment. Nobody moved. The only sound was the tick of the old wall clock counting off the seconds.

I was so glad that Rafferty had taken the girls outside. They would not have been quiet.

"Alright, both of you, that's enough. I will not have this disrespect in my home," Granny said, breaking the silence.

"You always take her side," Mom whined out, turning into her husband's chest.

"There is no side to take, Margot," Granny said. "I just get tired of this same old fight. You were a bad mother to Jessie, but you were grieving. Rita didn't have children because her body didn't allow it. Now, can we put this aside to eat? The food is going to get cold."

The two stood there, not speaking, not wanting to be the first to give in.

"Fine," Mom mumbled into Samuel's chest, then turned slowly, "Rita, I'm sorry."

Auntie Rita crossed her arms over her chest. "Fine. Me too. Sorry."

We all exhaled in a collective sigh. The fight was over. This time Auntie Rita won. She is almost always the one to apologize first.

I stuck my head out to tell the others dinner was being served. Sawyer became animated as he jogged to the door. He was always hungry, but he especially enjoyed it when my granny cooked.

"Everyone get washed up," Granny ordered as they came in.

The rest of us got the food to the table.

"It smells so good, Ines," Samuel said as he carried a platter of tacos.

We filled plates, then said grace before digging into the tacos, enchiladas, rice, and beans. Nobody spoke at the start of the meal, but as it went on people made small talk, especially the little girls.

"This is so good. I love tacos," Ivy said.

"I love the avocados," Dove added.

"Me too."

"And the rice."

"Oh, yeah, me too," Ivy grinned, shoving a fork full of rice into her mouth.

"I'm glad you are enjoying it." Granny smiled at them. "The rice is an old family recipe."

"Can you make it, Jess?" Ivy turned to me.

"I can."

"Oh, we need to have it for dinner every night," Dove declared.

Most of the adults laughed, but my mom rolled her eyes. I wanted to say something, but I wasn't the confrontational type. I glanced around the table to see if anyone else clocked her action. Auntie Rita caught my eye and gave me a nod.

Okay, I hadn't imagined it, I thought.

When everyone had finished eating, mom, Samuel, and my brothers prepared to leave.

"Thank you for having us, Ines," Samuel said.

Mom just nodded with a flat smile.

"Well, we enjoyed having *you*," Granny said. An emphasis on the you part, which I took to mean only Samuel.

I guess without my mother, he wouldn't be so bad. However, married to her, he was annoying. He didn't seem to have thoughts of his own most of the time. It made me sad for him.

"Bye, Samuel." I walked over, giving him a quick hug. It was so out of character that I heard a few muffled gasps.

"Oh, bye, Jessie," he said, tears in his eyes.

Once they were gone, Vee and I volunteered to clean up.

"I'll help you girls," Auntie Rita said. That meant she wanted to tell me something.

The rest of the group went into the living room to visit, and the girls said they wanted to show them a dance. We could hear them singing and giggling as we cleared the table.

"They are really so cute," Auntie Rita said.

"They're so fun. We love having them," Vee said.

"So, Jessie," Rita looked over her shoulder. "I assume you are looking into Samir's murder, yes?"

No point trying to hide it, and Auntie Rita had been a huge help in other cases. She had gotten me some great information.

"I am."

"Oh, good. I wanted to tell you what I heard about Anwar. I thought it might help."

"Anwar? From the Spicy Fig?"

"Yeah, how many Anwars do you know?"

"Okay, true. What did you hear?" I leaned in.

"He was seen over on James Street."

"James Street? Really?"

James Street was known as the place to get drugs, prostitutes, and place bets with bookies. It was not a place that most people I knew would go to. It was on the edge of town between Dashwood and Pinehurst.

"Yep, and that the person who shot Samir was actually looking for Anwar. Got them confused and killed the wrong person."

I immediately thought of poor Fatima. What if that person comes back? It had been more than a month now since Samir had died. They would have been back if that were true.

But to be fair, the family had been in Lebanon for almost a month, too. I really hoped it wasn't true.

"Where did you hear all of that?"

"From Anita Stone."

"Oh."

Anita Stone was Chief Cyrus Stone's wife. It was likely a credible source. Did he talk to her about all the cases? Was that pillow talk for them?

Then I thought of Kyle and our agreement not to share details of cases. I guess Anita and Chief Stone didn't have the same agreement.

But then again, perhaps Anita never stuck her nose in any of the investigations or been held at gunpoint.

"Yeah, I feel so bad for poor, sweet Fatima. She's in my book club and garden club. What a sweet family. Samir would sometimes attend with her, when he could get away from the restaurant. They were so in love."

"They seemed like it."

"I sure hope they find out who did it before anyone else falls victim to them."

"Me too."

"And me," Vee added.

"Also, you know that the leasing company is run by a loan shark, right?"

Vee and I both nodded.

"Well, that's all I know, but I'll keep my eyes open and let you know if I hear anything else."

"Thanks."

We finished cleaning the kitchen, then joined the others.

Chapter Nine

Last night, when we got home, I pulled the murder board out of the closet, writing James Street on the sticky with Anwar's name. Then I stared at the various clues.

We had all completely ruled out someone from his military service. That just didn't make any sense. I know it was important to Fatima. To her it might seem like this was yesterday, but really it was nearly forty years ago.

As I slipped on my shoes, I stared at the murder board in my closet. I could pretty much eliminate most of the suspects, because we knew it was someone with the leasing company, likely at higher levels.

The lower levels of the company operated normally, at least from my online research, that's what it looked like. Isn't that what they wanted it to look like? But I couldn't be sure without further investigation.

Even the police knew it was them, but they couldn't figure out who it was, despite having someone on the inside of the organization. Did they not have enough proof?

I wasn't going to pretend as if I understood what they were doing or why they were hesitating. I just hoped Zelda had some good information for me today and possibly would confirm that for me. But then what would I do with the information?

Once I arrived at work, I went about my normal routine as I waited on Zelda to call. She did as I was in the middle of chopping vegetables.

Of course, I thought as I wiped my hands so I could answer my phone.

"Hello?"

"Hey, Jess. I just parked. Ready for me?"

"Of course. I'll be right there."

I quickly washed my hands, drying them as I carefully jogged to the back door.

"Sorry, wanted to wash my hands really quick. Come in."

"Thanks, and trust me, I understand."

"I don't have my drinks up for service yet, but I do have coffee."

"Coffee sounds perfect. Black."

"Great." I grabbed a couple of mugs, filling them with the staff coffee, then handing her a mug. "Let's go out to the dining room."

"Your kitchen is great. So big and look at all the new equipment." She eyed it, then ran a hand over a stainless-steel work top as we walked by.

"Thanks. That's that TV money," I laughed.

I knew some of the chefs in town hated me for it and called me a sell-out. Others thought it was genius and wished they'd gone that way.

I gestured towards the closest booth.

"So, what's up? What couldn't you tell me?"

She cleared her throat, "Right to it. Alright. Um, so how much do you know about Klein leasing company?"

"Very little. Just that they are the ones who Anwar got their loan, equipment, and the building from. And that's who you use?"

"It is, well the equipment comes from another company, but they work together." She sat straight up, looking around. "You're the only one here, right?"

"Yes, just me and the alarm is set so we'll hear if someone else arrives," I said.

I did expect employees to start arriving soon. The next one to arrive would either be my maintenance person, Arlo, or Noah.

"Okay, well, I wish I wouldn't have gotten into business with them. At first, it seemed like a great deal. A building, help getting equipment, all the money I need, *AND* they would help me come up with the recipes. Where do I sign? It wasn't until the first payment came due that I saw just what was on the line. The interest alone means I'll never pay this off."

"But any loan would have interest. How bad can it be?"

"Well, bad enough that I am basically working for the sake of working. I pay each month, and I have not moved the needle on the principal loan at all. Plus, it isn't a fixed rate, so it is at their whim. If they want to charge me five percent one month and twenty-five the next, they do."

"That's not fair."

"Not at all. Plus, I can't hire my own employees, they hire them. They spy on me. That's why I couldn't talk the other day. I have no idea who is reporting back and who is just a regular employee, ya know?" She was shaking as she spoke. "I want out, but I can't get out."

"What happens if you were to quit? Leave the business?"

"I can't default, if that's what you are asking."

"I guess I mean, what if you asked them to sell to someone else?"

"They would loan to that person, but I still would be on the hook for at least part of the loan. It is a never-ending cycle for me."

"Oh gosh. I'm sorry."

"I love the business itself. The customers, being creative with flavors. I can add my own and you know I do. They just taught me the initial process and recipes, then I could take it from there. But the equipment they provided me with is subpar and is always breaking. I've gotten good at fixing the mixers and freezers."

"What about getting newer stuff? Do you have to use theirs?"

"Yep, it's in the contract that I must use the equipment from Avery West Equipment. That's the partner company," she added. "I suspect it's all stolen. The serial numbers and tags are all scratched off or removed."

"Oh my."

"Yeah, I'm not sure the benefit of stolen equipment. Maybe because it doesn't cost them anything."

"Yeah, that's probably it."

"You aren't thinking of getting into business with them, are you? I thought your business was doing really well."

"Oh, no, not at all. I'm looking into Samir's death."

"See? That's what I'm afraid of. If I don't pay, if I say anything, if I fight them in any way, they will send an enforcer. If I fight that person, you'll all be having a memorial for me, just like Samir."

"No. You think?"

"Remember that little diner on Carson Drive? Owned by that sweet couple, James and Talia?"

"Yeah, I loved that place." I gasped. "No!"

"Yep." She ran a thumb across her neck. "They both disappeared without a trace. Ask Chief Stone about it. It happened his first year as the chief."

"Do you think that will happen with Samir? Just an old cold case nobody cares about anymore." That made me sad to think about. Poor Fatima and her children.

"Probably. These people are powerful and hide in plain sight. Their business model, if you can call it that, is so complex that even if the police could find out who they are, it would take a genius or criminal to unravel it and prove guilty."

"Wow, I feel so naive about how things work."

"This isn't how things work. This is illegal and they need to be stopped."

The alarm beeped alerting us that someone had arrived.

Arlo's beautiful voice floated on the air. He had a gorgeous singing voice and often sang in Spanish as he worked.

"That's one of my employees, so I guess we are done, but thank you for the great information. It is really helpful."

She took my hand. "Please, please be careful. Looking into this group can be extremely dangerous."

"I will and you be careful, too."

I walked her out, watching her as she got into her car. Thinking about her words as I got back to work, this really did sound like an awful company.

That afternoon, I picked up the little girls from school.

"Hey, girlies. Buckle up," I said.

"Ohmygosh, I had the best day!" Ivy started to say, but two firetrucks, an ambulance, and a couple of police cars all flew past.

"Where are they going?" Dove asked.

"No idea," I said, watching them. I wonder if one of those cars was Kyle. My heart thumped as I said a silent prayer for everyone's safety, but especially for his.

The girls chatted all the way home. We went about our normal afternoon routine of them eating a snack and then doing homework. I listened to them both read and then I started making dinner.

The door flew open and in came a frantic Shayla. Luckily the twins were playing in their room.

"Did you hear? I can't believe it but We Scream Ice Cream is gone. Fire. One employee didn't make it out," she said.

My blood ran cold. Was this because she'd come to see me this morning? Had *they* found out? If so, they were much more powerful than I realized.

"Oh, my gosh. Do you know if Zelda … I mean, it wasn't her?"

"No, she's okay. It was one of the others."

"I need to call her."

I picked up my phone, then stopped myself. She was likely still dealing with the police and would be busy for a while. Instead, I sent her a quick message. No reply. Not surprising. It would likely be hours before she saw it, but I just wanted to offer my support.

The door opened and in came a breathless Vee.

"Did you hear about We Scream?" she asked.

"She was just telling me."

"Can you believe it?" Vee asked.

"Do we know what happened?" I asked.

"No, I just heard it because I work down the street," Shayla said.

"Post Office. Lots of news comes in," Vee said.

I felt a lump forming in my throat. "This is my fault."

"How is it your fault? Did you set it on fire?" Vee asked.

"No, but I pushed Zelda to tell me what was going on." I dropped my head onto the kitchen counter, letting out a groan. "She's going to blame me."

"No, she's not. It was the bad guys, whoever they are. Not you," Vee said, coming over to rub my back.

"Yeah, she knew there was risk, and she took it," Shayla said, taking a seat across from me at the island. She reached forward, taking one of my hands. I looked up slightly to smile at her.

"She will still have to pay back that loan," I mumbled, then filled them in on everything Zelda had told me today. Every shady detail.

"Wow!"

"Oh my!"

"Yeah, so now I feel responsible, even if she knew the risk, I pushed her."

My phone chimed. It was Zelda.

Z: **Thanks, Jess.**

Me: **It's my fault. Will you forgive me?**

Z: **Not your fault at all. I knew... I just want them to stop now.**

Me: **Let me know if I can do anything for you.**

Z: **Thanks.**

"I better go check on the girls. Let them know I'm here," Shayla said.

"They already did homework and their reading. I checked it all off."

"Thanks, Jess. You're really the best." She smiled as she skipped off to find her sisters. They squealed when she made it to their room.

Vee and I exchanged smiles.

"I'm going to change. Be back in a few," Vee said.

It wasn't until after dinner that I finally heard from Rafferty. He simply told me he was still working and would talk to me later.

R: **Be careful, babe**

Me: **You too**

I stared at his words off and on, until I finally fell asleep, and dreamed of kitchens, guns, and fires.

Chapter Ten

I pulled into the parking lot of Klein Leasing Company then parked in a spot labeled visitor. It was right by the double glass doors.

I sat for a minute trying to muster up some courage. After what happened to Zelda's business, I was a bit shaken, but I had to know what was happening.

The building wasn't fancy. It looked like it was only two stories, all brown brick with plate glass windows. The large parking lot only had a few cars. That led me to think, the building was mostly empty, but who knows what else they used it for if not offices for employees.

These people likely killed Samir and set a fire to Zelda's place. Now I was knowingly going in here to talk to them, possibly putting a target on my back.

Who am I kidding? I probably already have a target on my back. They know I have discussed this with both Fatima and Zelda.

Oh, bleep! I hope Fatima and her family are safe. Maybe I should check on her.

For now, I needed to get inside for my appointment before anyone got more suspicious.

The overcast sky opened up just as I got out. I jogged the few feet to the door, but I was still soaked. Stepping in, I was blasted with the air conditioning which sent a shiver through me.

"Brr… Oh, hi," I said to the receptionist who was staring at me with her mouth open.

"Um, hi, Jessica Vasquez, yes?"

"Yes, that's me." I tried to dry my face with my sleeve, but it was no use.

"Here." She passed me a few tissues.

"Thanks." I only used them to wipe my eyes. "I'm here to meet with Penny."

"Sure, but first, the restroom is down this hall on the left. You *may* want to freshen up." She pointed to her left.

I looked down the dark hall. The only light seemed to come from the windows. No overhead lights at all. It was kind of creepy.

"Just down here?" I gestured.

"Um, yeah." She rolled her eyes.

"Thanks. Be right back."

"Take your time." Her tone was the equivalent of an eye roll.

My shoes clicked loudly down the empty hallway. My fight or flight reaction was yelling flight, but I pushed on. Water dripped from my hair onto my face. I had gotten soaked. As I stepped into the echoey and cavernous bathroom, I wiped at it.

The automatic lights came on making it appear not so scary, but then I caught my reflection in the mirror and gasped.

I rarely wore makeup, but thought today was a good day for it. Big mistake. Huge mistake. It was melting down my face.

I grabbed a few paper towels, dabbing at the mess. Glad I threw some makeup in my purse today.

"Now I know why she suggested I fix myself up," I mumbled to my reflection.

Minutes later, I was at least more presentable and looked less like something that came in from the swamp.

"Better," she declared when I walked back to her desk. "I'm Erin. I will let Penny know you're here. Please have a seat."

"Thank you. And thanks for the suggestion," I thumbed over my shoulder.

"We women have to look out for each other." She winked, taking a seat at her desk, then the clickety-clack of the keyboard began.

Wow, I might have underestimated her.

I took a seat in a plastic chair with my back to the wall so that I could see the entire space. There was a staircase on the right that led to the second floor and what looked like a lot of closed and dark offices. From here, it looked like it was just that, an office building.

After several nearly silent minutes, I pulled out my phone to pass the time. I began doomscrolling through the various social media sites, because my anxiety wasn't high enough.

After I'd had my fill of sad and gloomy news stories, I stopped on my restaurant's page. Cullen was sure doing a nice job of marketing. We got a lot of online engagement.

Today's special was honey-glazed salmon, and the soup was tomato basil. We had over a hundred shares and nearly two thousand likes and loves.

I smiled and gave it a love, too.

A door creaked from upstairs, then shoes clicked on the floor. I hoped this was Penny. I wanted out of here. Quickly, I shoved my phone into my purse, then straightened as a fiery red head came into view. She wore a navy-blue power suit and six-inch heels. She stopped at the rail.

"Chef Jess?"

"Yes."

"Come on up." Then she looked down at Erin. "Thanks, Erin."

I hesitated for a moment. Not sure I wanted to go far into this empty building, but I needed to know what was going on. When I reached the top of the stairs, she turned nodding for me to follow her down the hallway.

I looked around. There was no overhead light here either and most of the offices we passed were empty and dark.

"This building is large."

"Yeah, since Covid, most people work remote, but some jobs require a human." She smiled.

"Ah, yeah." Now, it made a little bit more sense.

"In here." She stopped at one of only two offices with lights on. "Want anything to drink?"

"No, thank you." I stepped in taking a seat where she gestured.

"Great." She sat across from me at the desk. "Now, Chef Jessica Vasquez, you said you are interested in a second location so you can open a ..." She looked down at her notes. "Oh, yes, a to-go or take-out style restaurant. Is that right?"

"Yes."

"And, despite the success of The Crock Pot and your run on the competition circuit, you're out for capital so you were hoping we could invest with you?" She tapped a pen on the paper as if daring me to lie.

"Um, yeah, I have some money saved, but it isn't nearly enough for the property rental, equipment, a few months of employee costs, inventory, etc. After opening The Crock Pot, I know how much it takes to start up and I simply don't have it now, but I think it is a good time to get a second location while my current is doing so well."

"I see." She sat forward. "Do you really think I don't know why you're here?"

"Um, I don't know what you mean." I tried to play it off, but I knew the jig was up.

"Fine, let's play it your way. Do you fully understand what comes along with an investment with us?" She put a lot of emphasis on the word investment, which caused an icy chill to run through my body.

"You'll loan me the money, help with a property rental and put me in touch with an equipment leasing company, yes? That's what I saw online and heard from a few others."

She studied me for a moment.

"You know about the … protections, right?"

"Protections? No."

"Anwar didn't tell you about that."

"Anwar? Anwar Saad? No, he didn't."

She let out a laugh. "You really think I don't know who you are or why you are here? You're the crime-fighting chef. Everyone knows you. Fatima came to you for help with finding Samir's killer. Well, honey it isn't us. We're in the business of protecting our assets. He was an asset to us alive. Now look. His business is closed, and it was successful because of him."

I stared at her, then shrugged. "Okay."

"Chefs are such cocky and arrogant people," she said with a laugh.

"We have to be."

"Why?"

"Food is needed to survive, but it also brings people pleasure."

Not sure where that raw confidence came from, but there it was. I was cocky and arrogant. She studied me while I sat there with my smug expression, or I hoped it came off that way.

"Fine. But before you come in here looking for trouble, why don't you ask first?" She pointed at me. "Ask yourself if it would make sense for us to get rid of a hot investment. For a brand-new restaurant, the Spicy Fig was making a decent profit. We know you ate there at least once a week, sometimes twice. As I said, he was more important to us alive and running his business."

I blushed but then straightened my back. Fake that confidence.

She continued. "There is a group, and I don't know who they are yet, out there trying to hurt our business. They are criminals. Find them, then we'll talk about this fictional second location."

"And that's the group you are protecting people like Anwar from?"

"Trying, but that night, with Samir …" She bowed her head. "That shouldn't have happened. I don't know where our surveillance went wrong or where the security guard was, but …" She cleared her throat. "The Saads are good people and that shouldn't have happened to them."

"I agree."

"Well," she pursed her lips. "I have a meeting shortly, so unless you really do want a new location or protection or whatever, I need to cut this short."

"Well, thank you for your time."

"Of course. I'll show you out."

But when we stepped out the door, there was a lady coming out of the office across from Penny's office.

"Oh, Penny, ready for the meeting?" the brunette asked, as she sized me up. She looked vaguely familiar, but it was a small town, even if we were on the Pinehurst side where most people lived in Pinehurst.

"Yes, let me just walk Chef Jessica out."

"Oh, Chef Jessica. I've heard about you." She stepped forward with her hand extended. I shook it. "I'm Marisol."

"Nice to meet you."

"Same."

"Alright, ready to go?" Penny said, pointing me forward.

We walked back to the top of the stairs where we had another awkward exchange as I descended the stairs alone. She stood there watching until I walked outside. No idea if at that point she walked away, but it was still raining heavily so I stood in the vestibule for a moment as I rummaged for my keys.

Hitting the unlock button on my fob, I then ran through the rain.

Bleep! I had finally started to feel dry.

At least I could go home and change before picking up the twins from school later. As I drove home, I replayed the conversation over and over in my head. Had I learned anything? Yes, but had it gotten me anywhere? No, but it sounded like I was on their watch list. That was a little disconcerting.

I shivered from either the wet clothes or the thoughts that flooded my brain. Did I need to hire someone for protection? Was someone out to get all the restaurateurs or just those that used Klein Leasing Company?

That was what I needed to find out.

When I got home, the stray cat that lives on our street was sitting on our stoop. He usually stayed on the other side of the road. I jogged out of my car and under the overhang of our townhouse. He didn't move, just looked up at me and meowed.

"Aw, are you wet and cold?" I bent down to pet him. He let me, which was a surprise, but then he started purring and rubbing against me. "Aren't you sweet."

I looked at our door.

"I wish I could let you in, but I'm not sure how Lulu would react to having another cat on her turf."

In response, he pawed at the door. He had never so much as given me the time of day before this.

"I'm sorry, Mister Kitty." I stood. I didn't know what to do. It felt rude to open it then shut the door in his face. "What do I do?"

He meowed, then pawed at the door again.

Lulu was spayed and up to date on all her shots. Except for the possibility that they would fight, there wasn't much other risk to letting him dry off in the house. Plus, I could get him to the vet later.

"Fine, but just until it stops raining." I opened the door and in he ran. I didn't even see where he went, but next thing I heard was frantic meowing in the girls' room. I ran in that direction to find Lulu and the stray rubbing against each other and licking the other's face. "Well, alright, you're friends. Fine. You can stay."

I'm sure the twins will be happy.

I grabbed a towel and started to dry our new guest off. Neither he nor Lulu liked me doing it, so I just left the towel, then watched as they both started rolling around on it.

"Well, okay."

When they were done with it, I picked it up to take it to the laundry room. However, I couldn't quite make myself walk away from the cute scene yet. I watched in awe as they cleaned themselves and each other. It was as if they were long lost friends finally reunited.

Maybe they had interacted through the window. I never noticed, but it wasn't like I was home all the time and I had no idea what she did in the house while we slept.

A shiver ran down my spine reminding me I hadn't yet changed out of my wet clothes, so I finally walked away. I glanced once more at the new friends.

I guess we have two cats now.

Chapter Eleven

"Wow, what a rush." Eli laughed at my right.

"For real. You did great keeping up." I smiled at him.

He had been working here a couple of months now and we were finally getting a rhythm like I had with Hannah. Hannah had recently been promoted to executive chef and we swapped days that we were in charge. On my nonexecutive chef days, I tried to do more managing, mentoring, and working on menu items.

It also freed up more time to investigate murders, which apparently was my new hobby or profession or whatever it was.

We both got to work cleaning our stations and preparing for the next round of orders.

"Hey, Chef," Ava said coming to my station. "Anwar Saad is here. I asked him to wait at the bar."

"He asked for me?" A sudden panic stirred inside me. *What could he want?*

"Yes, he did. He is mumbling to himself. Ripley is doing his best to keep him distracted."

"Um, okay. Let me just wash up. Out in a sec." I looked over at Eli. We didn't have any current orders, and he could easily manage things now, so I wasn't worried. "Eli?"

"I got you, Chef," he said with a nod.

"Thanks."

After I washed my hands and smoothed my hair, I made my way to the bar area. I saw Anwar right away. He *did* seem to be talking to himself, but perhaps he was just talking into earbuds.

I took a deep breath and prayed for strength.

"Hi, Anwar. You asked for me."

He mumbled something. I touched his shoulder causing him to jump.

"Oh, Jess, I didn't see you."

"You okay? You look awful."

"Gee, thanks. I'm fine. Just guilt. Guilt filled life." He dropped his hands to his sides.

"Um, was that why you came here? To tell me you have guilt?"

"Yes. No, well, kind of." He looked at me, tears in his eyes. "This is all my fault. My father, Zelda's place. All of it."

"How? Why do you think that?" I said softly.

"Because I signed those papers. My father knew nothing about them. He trusted me to take on the business side of things. He just wanted to make good food for people."

I didn't know what to say because nothing I said would take away his guilt.

"He did love to feed people," I finally thought to say.

A slow, sad smile formed on his face as if he was remembering.

"Yeah, and now Mona, Ayman, and my mother will never see him again." The smile was gone. "For myself, I don't deserve such a wonderful man in my life."

"Why would you say that?"

He whipped his head around to look at me. His quick action had Ripley stepping forward, but I lifted my hand, so he leaned back against the back of the bar.

"Have you not been listening?" Anwar said. "I caused all this trouble. And had mother not come to you, then you wouldn't have spoken to Zelda, and she wouldn't have talked to you. I ruined two thriving businesses."

"That's not your fault."

"Why do you think that?"

"You were just trying to do the best for your family. These people are the ones doing shady stuff. You didn't know what they were doing."

"Oh, but I did. I knew exactly how dangerous they were and that failure to meet the payments could result in ... well, I didn't know death, but violence of some sort."

That surprised me as I thought Penny said they were protecting people, not hurting them.

"Was this Klein Leasing Company?"

His eyes darted around the dining room. There were only a few diners left, including the monthly book club that met here. They reserved fifteen seats and came in after the lunch rush.

Lowering his voice, he said "no, not them. The others."

"The others?"

At that moment, there was an explosion outside, and we lost power. Gasps and startled screams went through the restaurant.

"What the bleep?" I said, turning.

"They know! I must go." He scrambled from the stool and quickly exited the restaurant.

I wanted to follow him to ask more, but it didn't matter. I had bigger problems as I had to figure out what happened to our power.

Noah came into the dining room.

"Any idea?" I asked him.

"There was a transformer outside that blew up. The power company knows."

"No estimated time?"

"Nope."

"Bleep!" I looked around. "Okay. Let's just … comp everyone their meals and those that haven't eaten, um, give them vouchers for next time."

"Got it. I'll start on this side?" Noah gestured to the far side of the restaurant.

"I'll take the book club."

An hour later, we still didn't have power with no estimated time for it to be restored, so I made the tough decision that we would close for the night. We cleaned up, Cullen posted online, and Noah posted signs on the door.

I couldn't help but wonder if Anwar was correct, they knew he was talking to me. Whoever *they* were.

I headed out to get the girls. Stepping into the parking lot, I stepped right into a wad of gum. *Gross*.

I hopped my way to the area near the dumpster to see if I could find something to scrape it off. Not finding anything, I just scraped my foot on the concrete behind the dumpster. Nobody would likely walk over here.

When I was satisfied I'd gotten it off enough to get in the car, I saw the power company working on the lines. I had been so distracted by the gum that I hadn't seen them at first.

Hopefully they would get our electricity restored quickly, so that I wouldn't lose too much food. Noah had a food order coming in the morning, but it didn't account for us losing anything we already had. We would have to make a decision about placing a bigger order if it didn't come back on soon.

Lost in thought, I drove towards the elementary school. As I came to a stop light, it turned green, but movement on the cross street caught my eye. A beat-up van was speeding towards me.

I had the green light, but I took my foot off the gas preparing to stop. They finally did just inches from the intersection. The driver's face was hiding by a glare, but I knew he was staring right at me.

I mumbled to myself and continued on, looking in the rear-view mirror as I did.

"What is going on today?" Everything just felt off this afternoon, at least since Anwar came to visit. Had he put some kind of curse on me or just some bad vibes?

I pulled into the pickup line at the elementary school and then a warning light came on my dashboard.

"My tire?" *What is going on*?

People started pointing out and mouthing about a flat tire. I nodded, then pulled into a parking spot instead of driving through the line. I got out to inspect the damage. Yep, flat rear tire.

Bleep!

I walked over to the pickup line so at least I had the girls.

"Where's your car?" Ivy asked.

"In the parking lot. I have a flat tire, so we'll need to call someone," I said.

"Oh, dear, Jess, you can use the conference room right up front to wait, if you'd like," Ms. Flowers, the assistant principal, offered.

"Thanks so much." I took the girls inside and we took seats in the conference room.

I stared at my phone a second. Who should I call? Rafferty? Vee? Sawyer?

"Are you calling Kyle?" Ivy asked with a giggle.

"I don't know."

"What about Sawyer? I love Sawyer," Dove added.

"Yeah? I'm glad. But no, I think I need to call Mr. Elias. He can change the tire for me." I dialed the number of Elias's shop.

"Elias Tire. Elias speaking."

"Oh, hey, Elias. It's Jess. Jess Vasquez."

"Hey, Jess! I know who you are. What can I do for you?"

"I'm at the elementary school with a flat tire." We only had one elementary school in town, so I didn't have to elaborate further. It was the same one we all had gone to growing up.

"Ah, of course. You still have that Toyota, yeah?"

"Yes."

"Alrighty, I'll load up a couple of tires that should fit and be right over."

"Great. We're waiting inside, so just call or text when you get here."

I sent Shayla and Vee a message to let them know we were delayed. I didn't want them to worry, especially Shayla, when she came home, and we weren't there.

S: **Do you need me to come get them?**

Me: **They are okay for now, but I'll let you know.**

S: **K**

V: **Do you need anything?**

Me: **Dinner ideas?**

V: **I'll grab something.**

S: **Thanks, Vee!**

Me: **Yeah, thanks, Vee!**

Then I did my best to entertain the girls while waiting. We played a few rounds of eye-spy then they showed me a new dance they learned. Once all the kids had been picked up, Ms. Flowers came to check on us.

"Y'all good?" Gloria asked.

"Jess has a flat tire. Mr. Elias is coming to fix it," Ivy told her.

"Oh, he's a nice man to come help. You know I went to school with him, just like I did with Vee and Jess."

"You did?" Ivy asked.

"Yes, and Sawyer and Kyle Rafferty."

The girls exchanged an amazed look. They couldn't believe it.

"Do you need any water or anything?" Gloria Flowers asked.

"No, he should be here any minute but thank you," I said.

As if on cue, my phone rang.

"And there he is. Thank you." I answered the phone. "Hi, Elias."

"Hey, Jess. Just pulled in. I'm looking at your tire. I think you should call Raff."

"What?" I gestured for the girls to get their stuff and follow me. "I'm on my way out."

They skipped along with no sense of urgency, but why should they? They didn't understand adult problems, at least not car trouble. Some days I wish I could go back to a more innocent time.

"Hey, Jess." He leaned forward kissing my cheek. "You look wonderful. Hey, girls."

I looked down. I was still sweaty and gross and still dressed for the kitchen. They giggled at his acknowledgment of them.

"Thanks. You too." No point arguing.

"Okay, so you see here?" He pointed. "It looks like someone cut and scraped at your tire. Unless you hit something, I think this was intentional because of how almost perfect the cuts are. They didn't puncture the inner tire, so it was meant to blow out over time. Likely at a bad time."

I looked down at the girls. Darn, they were really paying attention to what he was saying. I wish I had asked Gloria to keep them inside while I dealt with this, but how could I have known someone was trying to sabotage me?

"Really? I didn't hit anything. Not that I remember."

"So, someone did this to you."

"But, who?" Though I had a few ideas.

"No idea, that's why I think you should call Raff or maybe Detective Upton."

"Okay." I pulled out my phone.

Gosh, I didn't want to make this call. Kyle would be worried, and Upton would be furious. He would know I was still investigating this case. I hit the button for Kyle.

It rang and then his deep voice came over the line. At the sound, a lump formed in my throat. It had taken years, but I had finally found my safe place. It was Kyle Rafferty.

We hadn't even said that we loved each other yet, but I knew at that moment that I did. I loved him.

"Hey, Jess. What's wrong?"

"Hey, um, I'm at the elementary school picking up the twins, but I have a flat tire."

"Did you call Elias?"

"Of course. He's here." I started crying. Elias took the phone. He relayed the message to Raff and then hung up.

"Okay, he's on his way." Elias handed me the phone, then hugged me. "It's okay. Sometimes this happens."

"I have just had a weird day." I sniffed, trying to fight the last remaining tears back. Ivy and Dove started sobbing. "Oh, gosh, I'm sorry, girls. Don't worry."

"You never cry!" Ivy said as her cries intensified.

Dove wrapped her arms around her sister. They were used to comforting each other. I bent forward hugging them both then tried my best to explain.

"I'm just having a bad day. Everything is fine. I promise."

They slowly stopped crying, wiping their eyes, and flashing me a sweet smile.

"Okay, better?" I asked.

"Yeah," they said, but they still looked a bit shaken.

I would have to wait until later to have my mild meltdown when I was alone and nobody would know. Crying could be cathartic, therapeutic. I was long overdue for a good, healing cry.

Elias entertained the girls while we waited for the police to arrive. Teachers checked on us as they left for the day.

It was roughly ten minutes later that Kyle pulled in with his sometimes partner Officer Tommy Roberts and a second car pulled in behind with Detective Richard Upton. His face told me all I needed to know.

The girls cheered when they saw Raff and started to run to him. I whispered that they should wait, because he was here for work. They nodded but giggled and waved at him. He smiled and waved back but was in cop mode.

"Well, well, well. Jessica Vasquez," Detective Upton said walking over. "What do we have here?"

They examined the tire, and Elias gave them his assessment of the situation. Rafferty looked at me halfway through, his forehead ceased with concern. I could tell he was fighting the urge to both lecture me and hug me closely.

"So, you didn't hit anything?" Raff asked me.

"No. I didn't even bump a curb."

"Tell him about your bad day," Ivy said poking my arm.

"What bad day?"

"Oh, just little things all day. The power is out at the restaurant. I stepped in gum then a red-light runner, well almost a runner. He stopped just before but then stared at me like it was my fault. My light was green."

"I can pull the camera if you want."

"No, no. It was just one of those silly things but all together, I just want a glass of wine and my cats."

"We have a new cat," Dove blurted out.

"Oh, yeah?" He already knew but pretended not to know.

"Yeah, his name is Baxter. He used to live outside," Dove said.

"I named him." Ivy grinned.

"No, I did."

"You both did," I said.

"Yeah, he is so cuddly."

"Lulu loves him."

Yes, she did. I guess they had become friends through the window over the years. She had forgotten who she was and only spent time with Baxter now.

Detective Upton and Officer Roberts said something to Elias who started jacking my car up to begin changing my tire.

"We are going to take this into the precinct to have the lab run for prints or any evidence. It does look deliberate. The cuts are too precise," Upton said.

"Okay, thanks."

He looked down at the girls, then at me. "I'll call you later with details." He smiled. "Hey, girls. Do you want some stickers?"

"Yes!"

He went to his car and pulled out some different little bear stickers. They were dressed up as police officers, fire fighters, and various other professions. They each picked a sticker and said thank you.

The officers waited around while Elias finished the tire and then once the bill was settled, we headed home. I would be so glad to put this day to rest.

Chapter Twelve

I lay in bed, staring at the ceiling. Last night, I'd had a good cry before falling asleep. Rafferty had called me late giving me a lecture about being nosy. It wasn't a mean or angry lecture, but it got the tears started. Then it just kept coming, long after we got off the phone.

Thought after thought brought a new batch of tears.

Thankfully, everyone was in their own rooms so nobody heard me, or at least I hoped they didn't.

Now this morning, I felt refreshed, stronger, and ready to jump in with both feet.

My plan for the day was to go talk to some of the other restaurants, ones I knew were using Klein Leasing. Perhaps they would be willing to shed light on what exactly is going on. I only had bits and pieces of it.

Talking to Penny made me question the leasing company as a suspect. She even flat out said it wasn't them. Though I still had some doubts.

But her words had me thinking it was someone else, but who? Who else did all these businesses use? Who else was a threat to them?

The only other company I knew they had in common was Avery West Equipment Leasing and Sales. That's where Zelda and Anwar had gotten their kitchen equipment from.

I dressed in my Neal Barney Bigfoot shirt with my black flowy skirt, black tights and my lace-up boots. I added a gray chunky sweater and silver jewelry.

"Wow, don't you look nice," Vee said at my door.

"Oh, hey, I thought you'd gone to work."

"Nah, government holiday."

"Oh, right. I forgot."

"Need a ride or die today?"

"Always!"

It would be nice to have her along for the ride. I'd be more confident with a partner, and she always asked great questions.

"Let me get dressed and I'll be ready in two shakes." She turned, jogging to her room.

Minutes later, we were on the road heading to A Dash and A Pinch. They served brunch starting at 9 am, so we would be a little early, but only just a minute or two.

"What are we doing so, I know?" She said, rubbing her hands together.

"I'm just going to see if I can get a feel for their lease and who else they might be working with besides Klein."

"Do you think Archer or Irene will be there?" Vee asked.

They were the owners and sometimes Archer cooked, but they weren't always there now that they had children. They left the running of the bistro to their staff.

"I hope so, but even if they aren't, perhaps Monica will know something."

"She's an awesome manager."

"Yeah, but Noah's better." I chuckled as I pulled into a parking spot a few spots down from the front door. A line was starting at their front door. "Already getting busy."

"Probably the government holiday."

"I wonder why the schools weren't out."

"No idea."

We got in line, just as they started letting people inside. When they got to us, we asked to be seated outside. I thought the cars and outside noise would muffle some of what we talked about. Plus, it was a beautiful day. Just warm enough to be comfortable with low humidity, so not sticky.

"Hey, I'm your waitress Ashley. Oh, hey, Chef Jess. Welcome in."

"Hey, Ashley. Good to see you again."

"Yeah, it's been a minute. I was sorry to hear about your date that time."

She was referring to the time I came in for a blind date and thought I had been stood up. Turns out, he had been murdered on his way to meet me. I had such a bad dating life history. Thankfully that was all behind me.

"Thank you."

She took our drink order and left us to review the menu. When she returned with our drinks, we ordered and then sat making small talk and observing the restaurant, staff, and customers. I didn't want to ask for the owners or manager yet. I didn't want to raise suspicion.

As our food came out, I saw Monica moving through the dining room, stopping at tables and visiting with customers.

"Looks like Monica is making the rounds," I whispered.

Vee casually smiled, taking a bite of her food, then looking over her shoulder. It was so nonchalant that had I not known what she was doing, I would have missed it. She was the best person to take on a stake out. Wait? Was this a stakeout?

"Yep, looks like she will be coming outside any … oh, now." She took a quick bite of food and looked at the street. "This is good."

"Hey, Jess, Vee. Thanks for coming in," Monica said as she came to our table.

"Hey, Mon. Good to see you," I said.

"Hey!" Vee grinned. "Wanna sit for a sec?"

"Um," she looked around. "Yeah, just for a second. How's your order? Good?"

"Very good."

"Excellent."

"Love to hear it. How are things over at The Crock Pot?"

"Wonderful. Busy. Like y'all, we have a line at opening time."

"It's a good feeling, huh?" She grinned.

"Very good. Beats not having business."

"Yeah, like that one place at the end of West Street," she said.

"Oh, I know. There one day, gone the next."

"Well, I better get back to it." She started to stand.

"Wait, just had a quick question for ya." I lowered my voice. "Besides leasing from Klein, who else do y'all do business with?"

"Oh, my. Um, you know I can get in trouble for saying anything. Look at poor Zelda and the Spicy Fig." She looked around almost frantically.

"I'm sorry to ask. I know it can get you in trouble, but just a company name. Is it Avery West or someone else?"

"No, I can't. I'm sorry." She plastered on a fake smile. "This meal is on me. Thank you for coming in."

She went to talk to Ashley who came over shortly after to confirm that Monica was picking up our tab. I had guilt now.

"That didn't go well," I mumbled to Vee after Ashley had walked away.

"I know."

We ate quickly and then left a big tip. I thanked Ashley and Monica as we walked out. Back in my car, I stared straight ahead. I didn't think it was going to be this hard to simply get a name.

"I just wanted a company name. I didn't ask anything else."

"I know. She panicked at just that."

"Right? What is this all about?"

"Well, now what do we do?"

"We have a few hours before the rest of the restaurants open."

"So, what's that mean?"

I looked at her. "Want to go to the comic shop?"

"Heck yeah! Always."

We killed time at the comic book shop. Monte had gotten a new shipment of the figurines that Vee liked, so while she looked through those, I walked along the back wall with local art displayed on it. Nothing caught my eye today, mostly because my mind was so distracted.

Around eleven, we headed over to Beaks and Brews. It was at this point that I realized a flaw in my plan.

"Nathan isn't going to have time to talk to me. He's going to be working, and I don't know if I can eat again this early," I said, as we sat in the parking lot. "We just ate that big breakfast."

"I know, me neither." Vee patted her stomach. "Still full. So, what's the plan?"

"Let me just see if he's cooking or if he is out in the dining room. Sometimes he's just walking around and letting his other cooks work the kitchen."

"Okay."

As predicted, Nate was walking around checking on customers, laughing with them, and refilling drinks. He saw us, gave me a smile and a nod as he made his way over.

"Hey, ladies. How's it going? Table for two?"

"Um, not today. Just wanted to see if you had time for a quick chat."

He looked around with a smile, then leaned in close to me, his eyes hardened. "You and I are friends, Jess, but I am not answering questions about what happened at We Scream, or the Spicy Fig. Got it?"

He forced a smile to his face, but his eyes were chilling.

"Well, thanks, Nate. I hope you have a good day," I said as bubbly and cheerful as possible.

We practically ran back to my car, jumping inside and slamming the doors. I could see Nate standing near the window watching us. I put my car in reverse and got the heck out of there quickly.

Vee and I didn't speak until we were two blocks away.

"Wow!"

"Yeah, wow!"

"Do we keep going?" she asked.

"Yes, absolutely, yes. Do you see how scared and different all our friends are? These are nice people. People we have both known for years. I need to figure out how to break them out of this fear."

"Okay, who is next?"

We drove from restaurant to restaurant, getting more or less the same reception at each. The owner, chef, or manager would be happy to see us then when we'd ask our question, they would shut down and rush us out.

"Wow. That confirms something is going on and they all know about it," I said.

"Yeah. It's sad and scary," Vee said.

"That was the last one on the list. We still have time before we need to pick up the girls. Wanna grab a coffee at Roasted Beans?"

"Sounds good."

We pulled in minutes later. It was quiet at Malory's shop, so we didn't have to wait for coffee.

"Oh, and can I get a slice of lemon cake?" Vee asked Malory.

"Of course!" She grabbed it, placing it on a delicate white plate with small pink roses painted around the edge. It was beautiful.

"Anything else?"

"That's good, Malory. Thanks," I sighed.

"You okay, Jess?"

"Yeah, just a frustrating day."

"Samir's murder?"

My head snapped up to look at her. "Yeah, how do you know? I didn't think you were involved with *them*."

"Oh, I'm not, but I know about it. Zelda and I had long conversations."

"Really? I had two conversations with her, and they burned her place to the ground."

"Yep. To keep her in debt to them and show her who is the boss."

"Who is it?"

"Birch Investments is who I suspect."

"Really? Not Klein?"

"Nah, they're just a cover. A way for the investment partner to launder money in a way."

"See? I heard the same thing, but I thought laundering involved cash businesses."

"It used to. Now it is mostly just a legit business to cover up illegal things, like drugs or inflated investment opportunities."

"Meaning?"

"Meaning they tell people with money that they can get more, and people without money that they will get some. In the end, the only one getting money is the higher ups."

"That isn't fair," Vee said.

"That's why it's a crime."

"Do you happen to know any other business she was working with?" I asked.

"Um, she was getting all her equipment through Avery West Equipment Rental. I wouldn't be surprised if they weren't in on this somehow."

That's the name I was hoping to hear today, but I didn't want to mention it. I needed someone else to say what I was thinking.

"Oh my gosh, Mal, you are a lifesaver. Thank you for this."

"You're welcome. By the way, I hear a lot of meetings over coffee, so if you ever need details, I'm your girl."

"Excellent." I paid, leaving her a big tip on the receipt. Then Vee and I took a seat by the window.

"We probably should have started out the day here." Vee laughed.

"Yeah, now I know."

With that bit of knowledge, we enjoyed our coffee, and I stole a bit of Vee's lemon cake. When I got home, I wrote the two company names and put them on the murder board that was still stashed in my closet.

Vee came bursting in holding her tablet. "Okay, I looked up both companies. Avery West Equipment Rental has some shady people working there. Look."

The pictures of the CEO and the CFO showed men with face tattoos consistent with a prison gang. I had seen those same ones numerous times when I'd visited my father.

I believe in second chances, for sure, but sometimes if it looks like a duck and quacks like a duck, it's a duck.

"I wonder what they were in prison for," I mumbled.

"Yeah, I was wondering the same."

"It really doesn't mean much though. Look at Smokes. Great guy but did time."

"And he's cute, even with the face tattoo."

"Vee!" I laughed. "What about Max?"

"Meh. I'm off him, back to Elias."

"I can't keep up with your love life."

"It's not love. Just fun to go to dinner and talk to someone cute."

"Okay. If you say so."

She rolled her eyes. "So, do you think your dad would know anything about this?"

"He might. He is pretty plugged in at Milton."

"So?"

"Yeah, I need to go for a visit anyway."

"Let me know if you want company for the ride, and I'm happy to take off a day."

"I'll let you know."

Chapter Thirteen

"I got the downstairs cat litter box cleaned up!" Ivy yelled.

"I'm finishing the upstairs one!" Dove yelled from upstairs.

"Great. Y'all are doing good," Shayla yelled from somewhere in the house.

I was in the kitchen. I had already washed the breakfast dishes, wiped all the surfaces, and was just finishing with the floor.

We were doing our weekly deep cleaning. Of course, during the week we cleaned all these things, but this included cleaning all the other things we didn't do daily.

Plus, we were having a house full of company over for a late lunch or early evening supper, however you wanted to look at it. We had Sawyer, Riley, and Rafferty coming. Plus, Vee had invited Elias. I didn't know what the story was here yet.

I know she has been out with Max but had also been talking with Elias. I don't know when things switched for her. All she had told me the other day was Max was out, and Elias was in.

"Laundry is in the dryer," Vee yelled.

"We're almost done!" Ivy ran in.

"Yes, you girls are being extremely helpful," Vee said.

They ran to the kitchen and climbed onto the bar stools. "Can we help cook?"

"It's not quite time for that yet, but of course you can."

"Yay!" They laughed and cheered.

"Go play in your room for now," I laughed, shooing them out of my way. "I'll call you when I'm ready."

They ran off, laughing and cheering. The adults finished up and plopped down on the couch for a quick break.

"The place looks good," Shayla said looking around.

"Yeah, I love our weekend deep cleans." Vee sighed.

"Me too. And it will be good to see Sawyer later."

"Not Riley?" Vee chuckled.

"And Riley." I laughed.

"Still not a fan?" Shayla asked.

"Um, let's just say she's grown on me some."

"Anything new with the case?" Vee asked.

"Nothing and I haven't heard about my tires either. I'm hoping Raff will give me some information today."

"Let's hope," Vee said.

We were quiet for a moment. The little girls were talking in their room. It sounded like they were acting out a scene from a movie they had recently watched.

"That's so cute." Vee giggled.

"They're so happy," Shayla said with a wide smile.

"I'm so glad they are getting to be little," I said.

"Me too."

"Yes, me too."

My phone rang. It was Rafferty.

"Hey, you on your way?" I asked.

"No, unfortunately not. We had a call about a homicide and even though I'm not on call, Chief wants me on it."

"Because you put in your application for detective?"

"Yeah, wants me to ride along with Upton on this one."

"Well, that part is kind of exciting, though a sad reason, I'm sure." I wanted to ask him more, but I had to honor our agreement.

"I know what you are wondering, and I can't tell you right now, but I'll call you later."

"Okay. Good luck."

"Thanks."

With that, we ended our call.

"Not coming?" Vee asked.

"No, they have a homicide, but he didn't give details."

"Oh bummer."

"Should we get started cooking?" I asked Shayla.

"Yep." She stood. "Hey, girls, time to cook!"

They came running out. I was happy to see the blossoming new generation of chefs, or at least a strong interest in cooking. I wanted to pass down what I had been taught by my grandmother and aunt. It was so satisfying to take a pile of ingredients and turn it into something delicious.

We worked on a big Italian feast of meatballs, tomato sauce, and two different pastas with a salad and homemade bread. The house smelled so good as things started to come together.

There was a knock on the door just as we were putting the bread in the oven.

"It's Sawyer!" Dove yelled.

"Can we answer it?" Ivy asked.

"I'll go with you," I said. Just in case it wasn't Sawyer.

I let Ivy open it.

Both girls squealed with delight to see it was their favorite guy.

"Sawyer!" They both yelled jumping at him.

He growled like a monster causing them to yelp and run away laughing. He came bursting in chasing them around. They ran and squealed with laughter.

"Hey, Riley," I said, gesturing for her to come inside.

"He has been so excited to play with them." She laughed.

"He is going to be a great father someday."

"Not just some day," she said, handing me a picture.

"Oh, my gosh! Really?"

"Yes. Due in about seven months. We just found out." She touched her stomach.

"Oh, my gosh!" Vee rushed over. "I'm so happy for you guys."

"Congrats."

I looked over at my best friend from middle school. He was still chasing the girls pretending to be a monster. They were laughing and howling with joy. He was going to be a wonderful father. He was always so patient, caring, and seeing him with children would melt your heart.

However, I couldn't help but feel a little sad. He had already moved out, but this really solidified that our threesome of him, Vee, and me were over. He had found his person, and they were starting a new life.

"So, give us the details," Vee said, pulling Riley into the kitchen. "Do you need a drink or something to eat? Are you hungry all the time? Oh, wait, are you feeling sick?"

"If you let her talk, she might answer a question."

"Oh, sorry. Go ahead. I'm just so excited."

Riley laughed. "Water would be great. My stomach feels okay. I'm nearly ten weeks. We just heard the heartbeat this past week. Not planned, but not exactly not planned. We are very happy."

She looked over at Sawyer. He had the biggest smile across his face as they made eye contact. It made me happy that they had found each other and were happy together but still couldn't help feeling a little sad for myself. It was selfish, I know, but overall, I was so happy for my friends.

Then I thought of Kyle. It had taken us a long time to find our way to each other, and I had hope that we would have a future together.

There was a knock at the door. Vee let out a muted squeal as she tried to control herself.

"It's Elias." She ran to the door. "Hi, come in."

There was a collective greeting from the group to Elias. He waved, but his focus was on Vee.

I swear my friend was blushing. She was not this excited when Max picked her up for their date. I'd have to ask her about it later, but for now I tried to refocus on what Riley and Shayla were discussing.

The girls were telling Sawyer about the new cat.

"His name is Baxter!"

"He's so cute."

"He has a little bite out of his ear, but the veterinarian said, that's an animal doctor, by the way. He said that Baxter is super healthy."

Sawyer was such a good sport not to tell Ivy that he actually knew what a veterinarian was. He simply nodded his head.

"Yeah, super healthy," Dove repeated.

"Well, I'm sure having two cats in the house is fun," Sawyer said.

The buzzer sounded for the bread.

The girls cheered. "Bread's ready!"

"Does that mean it's time to eat?" Sawyer asked them.

They looked at Shayla and me. We both nodded. They led the way as we filled plates and headed to our dining table.

"We set the table," Ivy said.

"Yes, you have to find your name." Dove pointed.

"Oh, fancy, fancy," Sawyer said, as he started looking for his name. "Oh, here I am. Right next to Riley and Ivy."

"And I'm across from you," Dove yelled, as she ran around the table to her seat.

There had been much discussion about seating arrangements. With them both wanting to sit next to Sawyer, this was the compromise so that they both could sit close to him. Of course, this was also before we knew Rafferty was going to be working so I had pacified Dove by telling her she could sit by Raff.

Thankfully, she didn't seem to miss him now.

However, I was missing him terribly as I watched my friends with their dates. I looked at the empty chair next to me, but trying not to let it spoil the fun afternoon with everyone else.

After the food was eaten, the girls talked us into a game, but with so many of us we couldn't play their usual board games that were made for only two to four people.

"Do you know how to play charades?" Sawyer asked them.

"Oh, oh, oh! Is that were you act out the things?" Dove said jumping up and down.

"That's it. Does that sound fun?"

"Yes!"

"Okay. Let's divide into teams with you two being the team captains." He looked up with a grin. He was brilliant. That should eliminate fighting.

They each took turns picking the person on their team and then we reviewed the house rules, so everyone was on the same page.

"Okay, I'm going to flip a coin to see which team goes first," Elias said as he pulled a quarter out of his pocket. "Heads is Ivy, tails is Dove. Okay?"

They both nodded.

"Heads."

"Yay, we go first." Ivy laughed.

From there we spent the next few hours laughing, guessing and arguing. I have played this game countless times in my life, but this had to be one of the best times.

"Well, I have to be going." Elias looked over at Vee.

She giggled and stood "I'll walk you out."

"We'll give them a few minutes, then we're leaving, too," Riley said, after the front door had shut.

"Bath time, girls," Shayla said.

"Can't we wait until they leave?"

"Please?"

"Okay, but only five more minutes."

The girls giggled and held on to Riley and Sawyer. Once Vee was back in the house, the visit was over and everyone left, and the girls went to take baths.

It was just me and Vee.

"So, what's up with you and Elias, and you and Max?" I asked.

"Oh, you know," she blushed. "Like I told you the other day, nothing serious. Just nice to have someone cute to talk to and hang with sometimes."

"It doesn't look like nothing. That blush."

"Oh," she touched her cheeks. "Is it that noticeable?"

"Yes, and not noticeable with Max as much as Elias."

"Max is great, wonderful, but Elias is just … I don't know. Amazing!" She giggled. "I am so over the moon."

"I'm so happy for you. Do you think he feels the same?"

"I think he does."

"So, you'll be the next one to leave our original trio, huh?" I teased.

"I don't know about that. What about you and Kyle?"

That was a good question that I wasn't prepared to answer, but it was fair for her to ask. After all, I had asked her first.

"Honestly, I don't know where we are. I mean it's comfortable. Like we've been together a very long time, but at the same time still so new."

"Well, you've been friends for a while."

"I guess, but I thought of us more as me being the pesky chef-slash-PI and him as the cop who was just trying to do his job." We laughed. "I felt more of a bother to him than a friend, this past year at least."

Before we could talk more, our front door alarm chimed on our phones, then less than a second later there was a knock at the door. We both exchanged a look before checking the camera app on our phones.

"It's Raff."

"And Detective Upton," I added.

There were also a few officers that I couldn't remember the names of. There was a recent graduation ceremony at the Pinehurst

Police Academy which the Dashwood department also hired from. They had added about six new officers.

We both went to the door.

"Hello, officers," I greeted them, trying not to make eye contact with Rafferty.

Whoops, I did. I felt my cheeks warm. He had that effect on me.

"Sorry to stop by without a call, but ... may we come in?" Detective Upton asked.

"Yes, um, please." I stepped back to allow them inside.

"Wait out here, Emerson." Rafferty instructed. "You too, Blair."

"Let me go let Shayla know, so she can keep the girls upstairs," Vee said.

I nodded, then turned to the remaining two officers, my boyfriend being one.

"Can I get either of you a drink?"

"No, thanks, Jess. Perhaps we can sit."

"Of course. Um, at the dining table?" I gestured.

"That works."

We took seats. Upton looked over at Rafferty who simply nodded then turned to me.

"Look, Jess, this isn't easy to tell you," Kyle's voice cracked. I wanted to reach out.

"Okay. You're scaring me."

"I'm sorry. That's why we brought those two officers. Wait, I'm getting ahead." He took a deep breath. It was the longest pause of my life. "The homicide victim tonight was the one who killed Samir. We don't know who killed him yet, but after accessing his phone with a warrant, of course, we found text messages of his ... umm ... services."

"Murder-for-hire," Upton added.

"Yes, a hitman. He had a contract for Samir, Zelda's employee, and ... now you."

"Me? Why me? I'm not involved in that ... that scheme or whatever."

"But you have been asking questions. I've warned you about this before," Upton said. His tone was calm, yet firm. As if he was talking to his children.

"We both have warned you." Rafferty's tone was more worried sounding.

"But, I just talked to friends, or people I thought were friends."

"These people are powerful, more powerful than friendship it seems."

"Also, your tire. We confirmed what Elias thought. It was cut to break at some point. We suspect it was meant to break at a different time, not just as a flat tire."

"What? Really?"

"Yes. When it failed to … um, kill you, that's when *they* came after this guy. We think he didn't actually want to kill you, so he did something he knew wouldn't," Upton said. "Of course, that's just what we are thinking. Unfortunately, he is dead so we can't ask him."

I just stared at them.

Raff cleared his throat, then said, "we want to tow your car so we can check to ensure everything is safe."

"Um, okay." I was struggling to process what they were saying. I heard it, but it just felt like a bad dream. It wasn't so much not having my car, I would rent one, but I was on a hitman's list. "So, you need my keys?"

Raff nodded. "Elias will be here any minute to take it. Do you need to get anything out of it? We might have it for a few days to up to two weeks depending on what we find."

I stood and walked across the room to retrieve my keys. I dropped them in Kyle's outstretched hand. Our fingers touched for a second, causing me to look up into his face. Big mistake, one lone tear slid down my face. He gave me a soft smile.

I took my seat again.

"Is there more?" I asked, afraid of the answer.

Upton sat forward, reaching a hand. "We are going to protect you. All of you. That's why we brought the officers with us today."

I could only nod. There was a lump in my throat threatening to spill more tears. I didn't want that, at least not until I could be alone. It was bad enough that one slipped in front of Rafferty.

"So, wait? Now what? What do I tell the girls about the officers?"

"We can have them in plain clothes if needed and they can just be hanging around as if new neighbors."

"The unit across the street is vacant."

"That might be something we could use," Upton said to Rafferty. "Let's look into that."

Raff nodded.

Vee came to stand by me. I'm not sure when she came in or how much she heard, but she wrapped her arms around my shoulder, squeezing me.

"We'll figure this out," she whispered.

I nodded, then looked at Rafferty as he and Upton stood.

"Are you able to stay?" I choked out.

"Unfortunately, we need to get back to the station so we can file reports, but..." He closed the gap between us, pulling me up and into his arms. "Please be safe. We've only just started this thing, and I really want to see where it goes. Okay?"

"Okay," I mumbled into his neck.

"I'll call you later. Okay?"

I simply nodded and tried to smile, but I'm sure it came off flat.

Vee and I walked them to the door. The two officers standing outside nodded. I heard Upton tell them to stand further from the house so as not to set off the front door alarm. He must have heard my phone going off randomly. I hadn't checked it because I knew what was causing it.

We closed the door.

"You okay?"

"No. You?" I asked her.

"No."

"What do we tell the girls?" I whispered as I could hear them coming down the stairs.

"We got to have a long bubble bath!" Ivy swooned as she walked down the stairs.

"It was heavenly." Dove copied her sister's dramatic pose.

Okay good, they hadn't overheard anything.

"Alright, little ones. Time for bed," Shayla said.

Vee and I quietly went to watch some television, which meant playing on our phones with the TV on in the background.

Shayla came out, looked at us both. "What the heck is happening?"

We summarized the best we could. I couldn't lie to her. She needed to know what was happening too, just in case she wanted to try to stay elsewhere for the time being.

"Wow, just wow." She plopped on the couch next to me. "Well, I've got your back. Whatever is needed or necessary."

I stroked her hair as I had done many times to calm her, but this time it calmed me. Maybe that's why my Aunt Rita had done this to me as a child, both to calm her and me.

"Thanks. Just keep you and your sisters safe."

"Can do."

Hours later, I paced the floor in my room. Both cats were on the bed watching me. They usually settled in with me to start the night, but at some point would move to either Shayla's room or the twins.

My phone rang.

"Hello?"

"Hey, beautiful. You doing okay?"

"Yes, are you still at the station?"

"Yeah, but I'll be leaving here shortly. Heading home so I can get a few hours of sleep."

"Okay."

"You sure you're doing alright?"

"Do you think I'm in danger?"

"I don't know, but the two officers who are there are some of our best."

"Okay. Okay."

"I'll call you again in the morning. Try to get some sleep."

"I will."

"Good night."

I stared at the phone long after we hung up. I did try to sleep, but I couldn't. Morning would be here before I knew it.

Chapter Fourteen

I yawned as I made my way down the highway. After Saturday night's news, I didn't sleep well in days.

But I'd promised my father I would come for a visit, and it was my only day off for this week, so it was my best chance to go. Not wanting to disappoint him by backing out, here I was yawning and sipping coffee as I made the roughly two-to-two-and-a-half-hour drive.

I was in a rental car, so it was a little strange. I missed my car and hoped the police department wouldn't find anything and that I would get it back.

Vee had offered to take the day off to drive with me, but I felt like I needed to visit him alone. Plus, it gave me a lot of time to think and overthink things.

Like why was someone out to get me? I mean, I knew why. They had something to hide and didn't want me messing up their business. Getting in between people and their money was a really bad idea.

But what I couldn't put together was why Samir was killed? What had he done to get in the way of their business?

Then, Raff and Upton had said Zelda's employee had been on the hit list. It hadn't clicked when they told me that, but then why had they burned down her shop? Was it to hide the murder? What had that employee done?

My guess was that the employee hadn't tipped them off to her talks with me, but someone else had. That's why they burned the shop to hurt her then killed the employee to send a message to others what they do if you don't follow their orders.

Just a wild guess, but it seemed to make sense, at least based on the limited amount I knew. Why else would they do it?

Now the hitman hired to take all three of us out had been murdered because he had not successfully killed me. He'd made a lousy attempt that obviously hadn't worked, and I was so thankful for that.

However, I now felt like it had put a bigger target on my back with these people. All I wanted to do was help a friend find peace in her husband's death.

I pulled into the long driveway of the prison. It was always sad to me to see the gray stone walls, razor wire coils on everything, cameras, and armed guards walking their patrol with my dad locked inside.

I parked in the visitor lot and then made my way into the visitor area to get checked in.

"Hey Jess, no treats today?" Officer Luna Pena asked as she waved me through the metal detector and then did a check of my purse.

"Not today, but maybe next time."

"I'm going to hold you to it," she smiled. "You're good. Enjoy your visit."

"Thanks. Take care."

I walked down the echoey hallway to the visitor's room. Years ago, we couldn't meet like this. Back then it was a room with stalls divided by glass. I liked this better. We could hug at the beginning and end of the visit, but other contact was limited. It was a far cry from when we couldn't touch at all.

I took a seat so that my back was to a wall, and I could face the door. From here, I could take in the whole room. It was the usual crowd, though not many visitors today since it was a Monday.

Still there was a young mother with her young children. One was running around screaming, banging on stuff, and just in general being a terror. The other child was an infant. She was crying and all the mother's attention was on the baby rather than the toddler.

There was an older woman at another table. She was reading a book while she waited. We made eye contact, smiling at each other for a moment before the buzzer sounded letting us know our loved ones were coming. We all straightened, except the toddler who continued to run around.

There were only about six prisoners in the line, so I saw my father immediately. His face lit up when he saw me. He gave me a quick little wave, then when they gave the okay, he rushed to me for a hug.

"My Jessie. You look so good. Did you lose weight or change your hair?"

"Um, no, nothing."

"Well, something is different. You have a glow."

Could it be because I was in a happy, healthy relationship? I wasn't sure if I was ready to share with him, but soon.

"You look good, too. You feel well?"

"Oh, yeah. I'm strong as a horse." He grinned. We took our seats. "So, tell me about what's going on? It isn't a holiday or either of our birthdays, why are you here?"

"Right to the point," I let out a nervous laugh. Lowering my voice, I said, "do you know anything about an organized crime ring in Dashwood, specifically when it comes to restaurants, leasing companies, anything like that?"

He sat back as he studied me, rubbing his jawline.

"You're talking about the equipment company scams, right?"

"Equipment company? I thought it was the leasing company."

Though I did have some suspicion about the equipment company, Malory had said she thought it came from even higher up, at the Birch Investments which was above them both.

He looked around, leaning in closely, and wagged his fingers for me to get closer too.

"There was a guy in here not long ago talking about it. He was transferred a week or two back. Anyway, he said they would go to the bigger cities like Pinehurst, Brighton, and Castle View, then break into the restaurants to steal things. Mixers, blenders, stoves even, anything they could carry and had the manpower to load. Then they lease that to other restaurants using steep interest rates, fees, and hefty penalties for missing payments, up to and including death."

"Death for missing a payment?"

"Shh, keep it down. You never know who is listening. That's why the ole boy got transferred. Too many connections here." He glanced around casually, before he continued. "But, yes, death for missing, well, more than one payment. If it became a problem, then …" He simply nodded.

"Wow."

His eyes narrowed on me. "And how are you wrapped up in this? You aren't considering doing business with these crackheads are you?"

"No, of course not. I am helping out a friend. They owned a restaurant in Dashwood. He was killed. They want to know by who and why."

"Well, be careful, Mija. These are not people to mess with."

"Is there anything else you can tell me about them? Like where they do business? Who else they work with? Who are some of the leaders? Anything."

"Not much more. Definitely don't know any big names, only guys like that one. Most of the time when they come in from that group, they're split up immediately. Too many fights. A few deaths taught the powers that be to not house this group together."

"What? Why? Aren't they on the same team?"

"Apparently, now mind you, this is just what I've been told, but they get like a commission when they bring in new restaurants and new equipment. They are often pitted against each other in huge rivalries."

I felt like the wind had been knocked out of me. This was complex, like Raff had said, and it sounded extremely dangerous. *What had I gotten myself into?*

"That's a lot to take in."

"I'm sorry. Maybe I shouldn't have told you."

"I'm glad you did. Now I have information about the type of people these are." Not that I knew what to do with it, but I would keep that part to myself. If someone made me guess who the killer was, I would say the equipment company. "What is the name of the equipment company?"

"Avery West Equipment and Machinery Leasing."

"Thanks."

Okay, that's the name I had, too, but I wanted to make sure it was the same.

"Now, Mija, let's talk about something else. How are you? Tell me about this Kyle guy your grandmother was telling me about."

I'm not surprised that Granny had spilled the beans, but I wish she would have let me share my news with him.

I began to fill him in on how we first met in middle school and then lost touch over the years, reconnecting when I opened my restaurant in town.

"He's an officer and working towards being a detective. He has started to study and is shadowing the lead detective now."

Well, technically Richard Upton was the only detective in Dashwood, but I left that part out.

I told him about how we kept running into each other, how he has stepped up when I've needed something. Then I told him all about how he asked me out the first time.

"He even kept an eye on Lulu while we were in Orlando for Shayla's competition."

"He makes you happy?"

My face warmed. "Yes."

"I can see. Wow! I'm happy for you."

"Thanks."

"How are the girls doing? Ivy and Dove, right?"

"Yes. They are doing so well. Shayla has found a therapist so they will start that next week. Most of the time, they act like normal eight-year-old girls then something will happen, and we can't get them to stop crying."

"Awe, that's to be expected. I remember that's what Granny would say about you. I was so thankful that she and Rita were able to take you in, just as you are helping these three sisters. Paying it forward."

"I hadn't thought of that. Not in that way before."

The buzzer sounded that the visiting time was over. We looked at each other. A sudden panic filled me. I wanted to grab him and hold on.

"Okay, Mija, I'm so glad you came to see me. I love you." He gave me a long, tight hug.

"I love you, too."

We kept eye contact until we could no longer see each other anymore. I hated this part. I always felt empty and alone as I walked back to my car.

When I used to come as a young child with my grandmother, she would make a stop at a little diner that was roughly thirty minutes outside of Dashwood called Rosie's Diner.

As I drove the car down the long driveway with Milton County fading in the rearview mirror, I knew Rosie's Diner would be my next stop.

Chapter Fifteen

I pulled into Rosie's just minutes before the lunch rush. My drink arrived just as the place started to fill up. They made their own sodas here, so I had to have a strawberry cream one. I also ordered a turkey club with their homemade fries.

"Anything else, Hun?" Nell asked. She had been a server here for as long as I can remember.

"No, that's good. Thanks, Nell."

"Anytime."

I messaged Vee and Shayla that I was done with my visit and had made a stop. I would still get home in plenty of time to pick up the twins and make dinner. Then I scrolled through my phone just to see if I had missed anything.

Nothing, just some more pictures of my mom, stepfather, and brothers living their best life without me. Not that I was bitter.

Okay, maybe a little, I thought, laughing to myself.

"Knock, knock. May I have a seat?" A woman's voice asked.

I looked up to find the lady who I'd seen after meeting with Penny. I wracked my brain trying to remember if I had been introduced and if so, what was her name?

"Um, sure."

But she continued standing.

"Do you remember me?"

"To be honest, I know your face but not your name."

"Marisol. I met you briefly at Klein Leasing."

"Right. I'm Jess."

"I know who you are. That's why I stopped at your table."

"Right, duh. Sorry. What can I do for you, Marisol?"

But before she could answer, Nell came over.

"You joining?"

"Yes, ma'am." Marisol slid into the booth. "Can I get … what did you get?"

"Strawberry cream soda, turkey club with fries," I said.

"Same for me. Thanks so much." She smiled at Nell, then turned to me with a frown.

"You got it, Hun." Nell walked away.

"Let me tell you who I really am. My name is Marisol, but it's Marisol Reyes and I work for Dashwood Police Department in the organized crime and homicide division, specifically as an undercover agent." Her voice was low, but her tone was sharp.

"Oh."

"Yeah, oh, and you are going to blow everything I have worked on for two years by your Scooby-Dooing around."

"Did you just use Scooby-Doo as a verb?"

She stopped and thought, cracking a brief smile before it quickly faded. "I guess I did. You understand my point, though, right?"

"Yes, I'm not trying to blow everything for you. I honestly just want to help my friends find closure and possibly reopen their business."

"I understand. I want that for them, too." Her tone softened. "I was close to finding out the hitman's name when he got axed. Now I'm back to square one because they will just send hitman number two which means I have to start gaining trust all over again."

"Trust me when I say, I didn't even know there was a hitman and to find out I'm on the list was the last thing I wanted." I paused. "Wait? How do I know you are really who you say you are? How did you know I was here?"

She pulled out her phone, hit a few buttons.

"Hey, it's me. Talk to her." She thrust the phone towards me.

"Hello?"

"Jess, you need to trust her. She's who she says she is." It was Kyle Rafferty.

"Kyle? But ... what is going on?"

"I knew you were going to visit your dad and asked if she could follow. It was less suspicious than our two uniformed cops going. Plus, she wanted to talk to you. Let you know who she was."

"Okay. Um, I don't know what to say."

"Say you'll be careful."

"I will."

"I'll try to come by tonight, but no promises."

"Okay. Talk later."

"Talk later."

I handed the phone back to Marisol. She wrapped up with Raff and then gave me an *"I-told-you-so"* look. She definitely did.

Nell came over to drop off Marisol's drink and just do a check on us. Once she had walked away again, I turned to Marisol.

"What do you need from me now?"

"I need you to be careful. Be smart. And most importantly, stay out of my way." She pointed a finger at me.

"Yep, can do. Definitely."

"Why do I feel a but coming on?" Marisol eyed me.

"But my name is on a hit list, and I am not just going to not find out who is behind this and why."

"You know why. You're asking questions and nosing around. That is why Samir was shot."

"You know that's why he was killed?"

"Yes. He came into the office to speak with Penny. I could hear what was happening from my office. He wanted to understand what his son had signed them up for. When he didn't like what he heard, he said he was going to contact the authorities and break their contract."

"Wow. I didn't know." I sat back hard against the booth seat. The vinyl squeaked and creaked slightly.

Marisol lifted a brow in my direction. I blushed.

"It was the seat."

"Yeah, this vinyl is pretty but not comfortable." She chuckled. "And, yes, nobody knows yet the motive. Well, Stone, Upton, and Raff know but no one else."

"Fatima and the family don't know?"

"No one else outside of the police department and when I say the police department, I mean those three and myself. Now, you." She gestured towards me.

"My lips are sealed." I did the key to lips thing.

"No putting this on your murder board."

My mouth fell open. "You know about that?"

"Yeah, and honestly, I like it. I do like your courage and savvy at figuring out these murders."

"Honestly, most of it is being in the wrong place at the wrong time, not actually me figuring it out."

"Upton says you have most of it worked out. Not bad luck." She tapped her head. "Smart."

I smiled at her compliment, but Nell brought our food before I could reply further.

"Enjoy, ladies. Let me know if you need anything else." She set a ketchup bottle in between us, then turned to head to the next table.

"This looks good," Marisol said, picking up the first triangle of sandwich. "I've never been here before."

"It's a family favorite, for obvious reasons."

"On the way back to Dashwood from Milton?"

"Yeah. I have been coming here for years. Not every trip but quite often."

We began eating, making small talk between bites. This was a weird relationship we had going on. Not a new, budding friendship, but not quite enemies either. If the situation was different, though, I could see us being friends.

We finished our meals.

"Those milkshakes look awesome. Have you had them?" she asked me.

"Of course. They are amazing. I usually get a double chocolate."

"Let's order two." She signaled for Nell and placed our order.

"Good choice. I'll get those right out."

"So, tell me about you, Chef Jessica."

"Um, what's to tell? You know about my father. I lived with my grandmother and aunt. I had a rebellious teen phase until I found cooking."

"For a second, I thought you were going to say Jesus." She laughed. "Not that there is anything wrong with finding Jesus. I'm a Christian myself. Church every Sunday, but I just thought that's what you were going to say."

"Ha, yeah, I can see that, but no, cooking was my awakening, if you will. It opened up a whole new world to me, friends, opportunities, and I finally had a purpose in life."

"That's awesome."

"What about you? What are you able to tell me about yourself?"

"Military brat so I don't have a home, so to speak. I then went on to serve in the Army for eight years. I traveled a little until I stumbled across Pinehurst and joined the academy. Worked there for a few years until Dashwood needed a female to work undercover. Enter me, and that was just a few years ago. Not much else to tell."

"Military sounds exciting. Go anywhere interesting?"

"Unless you like sand, not many. My dad was stationed in Germany and Japan, so those were kinda fun."

"I haven't been out of the country yet, but I have traveled quite a bit around the states."

"I have seen you on TV. You're really calm, focused. It is impressive. Is that how you run your kitchen?"

"I try to, but just like anything, it gets crazy, and I can lose my temper for a minute."

We continued the small talk and when Nell brought our milkshakes, we enjoyed the chocolatey goodness.

Nell dropped the bill off. "No rush, ladies."

"I'll get it," Marisol said, grabbing it. "After all, I ambushed you."

"No, you don't have to," I grabbed for some cash.

"Nope, any girl that puts up with Raff is good in my book." She gave a wink.

Wait? Did she have a thing for him? Should I be jealous or concerned about them?

"And don't worry, I think of him as a little brother, not a potential date."

"I wasn't worried," I said. Could she read minds? *I'm thinking of a number between one and ten.*

"Ready?"

"Yep." I guess she couldn't read minds after all.

We stopped at the cashier register where she paid, then we walked outside.

"I'll trail you on the way home to watch for anything unusual, but you should be good. Nobody followed you out here."

"Except for you."

We laughed.

"Yes, just me." Her expression changed to firm. This must be her cop look. They all had one. "I know we had a nice, buddy-buddy lunch, but remember what I said. Let me do my job and try to stay out of the way, safe, whatever. Okay?"

"I'll try." I think I had all the investigation done that I really needed to do. I just needed to study the clues at this point anyway.

"That look. Jess, you need to work on a poker face."

"Sorry."

"I mean it. Be safe and out of my way."

"Got it."

With that, we climbed into our separate cars and made our way back to Dashwood. I had a lot to add to my murder board. I really hoped the answer would be there, so I didn't have to worry about my safety or those around me.

But for the last thirty minutes of my ride home, I worked on my poker face instead of thinking about the case.

Chapter Sixteen

Minutes before we opened, I made my way around the dining room to ensure everything was set. I was working as manager so that Noah could be off today. Hannah was the executive chef for the day shift.

I tugged at the sleeve of my blazer, hating every minute of having to wear it, but I knew I looked nice and professional. It was the price of being a business owner.

Business owner. It still brought a smile to my face nearly a year later.

"Ready, Crock Potters?" Ava yelled.

There was a chorus of ready from all around the restaurant. She turned the key, then held the door for the early diners, greeting them all.

We got everyone seated with menus. Some already knew what they wanted, so we took their orders right away.

After seating a group of Auntie Rita's friends, I turned back to see a familiar face come through the door. He was followed closely by a young man who could have been a clone of the man in his younger years.

"Hello, Mr. Mitch. Welcome."

Mitch was a neighbor of Granny and Auntie Rita's. I met him a few months ago when Shayla's car had been vandalized in front of their house. He had been so sweet to let me in to view his security camera footage.

I had stopped by a few times since to bring him little treats or soup. He has so many wonderful stories.

"Oh, Chef Jessica. Hi, so good to see you," Mitch said, balancing on his cane and taking my hand with his other hand. "This is my grandson, Allen. He is in town, and I told him, do I have the place for you, so here we are."

"Yes, of course. Hi, Allen, nice to finally meet you."

"Nice to meet you, too. Grandpa has told me so much about you as well."

"Let's get you both seated over here." I put them at a table close to the front door, so Mitch didn't have to walk too far. "We have a special of roasted chicken today. Ava will be your server."

Ava walked up with a smile. I let her take over as I went to check the kitchen. I knew tickets would start coming back soon, and if they got bogged down within those first ten or fifteen minutes, I could assist on the line or help with running plates to the dining room.

Not that I didn't trust my staff, but it is what Noah always did. There were days that it was needed. Today was not one of those days, but it did make my body itch to get behind the cook top or stir the soup. Something.

At noon, another group of familiar faces came into the restaurant.

"Hi, Fatima. Nice to see you," I greeted her.

"Nice to see you, Jess. You remember my daughter, Mona, yes?"

"Of course. Nice to see you Mona." I looked behind them. "Your sons didn't come today."

"No, no. They are actually working to get our restaurant reopened."

"Really?"

"Yes, it is so exciting. We were able to get a different investment deal with a different investor. Legitimate this time. I want to tell you all about it. Do you have time to sit with us?"

I looked around. The lobby area was getting full.

"Not at the moment, but I will stop by once I get these folks seated and things slow a bit."

"Oh of course, of course."

Jordan got them seated while I helped the next group. As we got to the end of this group, there was yet another pair of familiar faces.

What is happening today? I thought as I plastered a smile to greet them.

"Penny. Erin. Welcome."

"Oh, it's Chef Jessica," Penny said. "No cheffing today?"

"No, today is manager duties day."

"Well, you look better than the last time we saw you," Erin snipped. "I love the blazer."

This lady ran hot and cold. I couldn't read her at all. It was a bit unnerving. She reminded me of that commercial for the sour candy. One minute sour, then the next she was sweet. I liked to know where I stood with people.

"Yes, well, no rainstorms today and I'm inside." I picked up a couple of menus and guided them to a booth. "Today's special is a roasted chicken, and Skye will be your server."

Skye stepped forward, but before she could take their drink order, Penny stopped me.

"Before you go, Chef. Is that Fatima Saad over there?"

"Um, yes it is," I said. Though I had thought about lying, where would that get me?

"I should go say hi. Excuse me." She crossed the restaurant before I could stop her.

Fatima smiled, but I could tell by her tense body language that it was a forced action. Should I save her? Thankfully, Penny was brief and rejoined Erin at the table.

"Poor thing. Still so tense," Penny said, picking up her menu.

I wished them well before walking away. Fatima caught my eye, flashing a weak smile, then averting her eyes. It must be unnerving to see their former leasing company representative here, especially knowing the shady business they were in.

We finished getting everyone currently waiting seated, then I made a quick round around the restaurant to check for any hiccups in service and ensure all the guests were happy.

Once I knew everyone was happy, I walked to Fatima's table. They were nearing the end of their meal, so I knew it was now or never. I stood in front of Fatima in an attempt to block Penny and Erin from seeing her.

"So, that's exciting about the restaurant. How did you get out of the lease with the other company?"

"Our new investor was able to find a loophole in the contract. I don't understand all the business bits of it, but Samir's death helped break the lease."

Mona made a slight whimper sound. We looked at her. She wiped a tear.

"Sorry, I miss him."

"We all do." Fatima took her hand, squeezing. "Father would be proud of you and happy to see his restaurant reopening."

"I know," Mona whispered.

I felt like a third wheel in their private grief, so I stayed quiet, until Fatima turned back to me with a smile.

"We will be having a grand reopening night. We wanted to invite you. It's in a few weeks. I'll send you all the details."

"That sounds wonderful. I will be there."

"You can bring your friends and of course Shayla and her sisters. There will be lots of children."

"Thank you. For sure, we'll be there. I'm so happy to see you both. Take care and I'll see you soon."

As lunch service started to slow, I went to stand near the bar. I could see the entire dining room from here. We still had a nearly full restaurant with tables in varying stages of service.

Penny and Erin were still here, but it looked like they were chatting as the check sat unpaid and untouched on their table. Their tense body language had me wondering what was so serious.

I was glad that Fatima and Mona had already left. Perhaps they were the source of the heated discussion or maybe it was just business talk.

Ripley dropped a glass of iced cold tea next to me. I had switched it up and wanted the peach iced tea today instead of my normal lemonade. I needed a little caffeine boost and a little less sugar than the lemonade.

Sipping it, I scanned the restaurant's remaining patrons. There was a group of ladies. I recognized some from my grandmother and aunt's church. There was the staff from the eye doctor's office across the street. They came over at least once a week, taking turns who would stay behind at the office.

Then I saw a lone man sitting at a booth. It was not unusual to have lone diners that would come in for their lunch break, but there was something about him that felt out of place. He looked up and our eyes locked. A slow, wide smile filled his face.

On the surface it appeared friendly, but it sent a chill down my spine. I looked around to see if anyone else had noticed or seemed startled by this man. No, no one. The world just moved around as normal.

I looked back as he waved me over. I couldn't refuse as I was the owner and manager, so I couldn't ignore a customer. Forcing my legs to move, I felt as though I was walking through wet cement up to my thighs.

"Hi, is everything okay?" I asked, plastering on my best customer service smile.

"Yes, wonderful. Wonderful. Great food, better service. I just wanted to tell you that."

"Oh, well, thank you." I breathed a sigh of relief. He was just a happy customer

"You're that chick chef that was on television, right?"

"Yes, I used to compete."

"Nice. Very nice. And, that's how you bought this restaurant, yeah?"

"That and a lot of hard work, yes." *Where was this going?*

"Well, good for you. I sell and lease kitchen equipment." He passed me his card.

His card read:

Michael Baller, Sales Manager
Avery West Equipment and Machinery Sales and Leasing

"Michael?"

"That's me. I go by Mike or just Baller." He winked. I fought the urge to shudder. "If you are ever in need of new equipment or want to sell yours, I'm your man. We deal in new and used, sale or lease. We do it all."

Oh, he was just a salesperson. Not a creeper, even though he really gave off those vibes.

"Nice. Thank you. I will keep you in mind. For now, my equipment is all brand-new, but this is helpful." I pocketed the card.

"Great. Anyway, just wanted to compliment you on a job well done." He stood and was about two inches taller than me, but the energy he gave off made him feel oh so much larger. He tapped the table where the receipt with his signature on it was left. "I have already settled. Take care."

With that he walked out. I watched him go, never turning back. He walked with a confidence that felt powerful and creepy at the same time. Once he was gone, I let myself shudder this time. Here on business or not, he had me in a paranoid state.

The rest of the day I was so jumpy. Smokes dropped a tray of plates, causing me to scream. Everyone looked at me like I'd grown two heads. Sure, being startled by a loud noise was normal, but I squealed like a piggy chased by the big bad wolf.

"Sorry, Jess." Smokes blushed. "I didn't mean to scare you."

"Of course not. I'm sorry," I said, as I helped him clean up the mess. "Just a little jumpy today."

Thankfully, the shift ended. I was never so happy to see Cullen in my life. We did the usual turn over and then I headed to pick up the twins from school. I sure hope they didn't have a lot of homework. I could use a good game of Candy Land, Sorry or some other board game with my two favorite girls. It might just calm my nerves.

Chapter Seventeen

"Chef, do you have those two specials ready?" Ava asked, waking me from my daydream.

"Oh, bleep, hold on," I said, as I pulled the steaks from the grill, setting them gently next to the already plated sides. "I'm so off today."

"Yeah, what's up?" she asked, leaning against my station. "Are you sure these are medium?"

I touched them lightly. "Yeah, they feel right. Sorry, I just have a lot on my mind."

"Samir and the Spicy Fig?"

"How do you know?"

"Chef, come on." She winked as she grabbed the two plates and left.

Yeah, I shouldn't be surprised that everyone knows. Nadine from *Dining with Nadine*, the online blog, had done a whole spread about me, not once but twice calling me the crime-fighting chef.

Then the local media latched on and now, everywhere I go these days people have these expectations of me. Look at how Fatima came to me to solve her husband's murder.

I really had a love-hate relationship with this whole thing. I loved the puzzle and challenge of it, but I hated the associated danger.

"Um, Chef?"

I looked around. Eli was pointing at the flat top behind me. Turning, I found a lot of smoke and a smoldering salmon filet. That wasn't what was supposed to be happening.

"Oh, no!" I grabbed the filet, flipping it off the cook top. "What is wrong with me today?"

"Why don't you take a short break? Get a drink or something. I'll take over." Eli smiled as he slapped another piece of fish on the cook top.

"Sure. Thanks." Sheepishly, I walked over to the sink. I washed up then headed to the bar for a drink. It seemed word had already reached Maxine as she had an iced cold lemonade waiting for me.

"Thanks, Max! Lifesaver."

I took the drink then made my way back to the office. I needed a little quiet for a few moments to refocus. Luckily, Noah was out in the dining room, so I laid my head on the desk.

I had been off yesterday and back in the kitchen today. At first, it felt good to be back to chopping, stirring, blending, but soon the weight of everything took over my mind. It was a lot.

With a threat hanging over my head and the hopes of an entire family waiting for me to find their father's killer, I wasn't sleeping much. My brain wouldn't shut off.

Focus on the tick of the clock. I told myself.

My body got heavier and heavier, then I don't remember anything.

"Chef?"

"Huh? What?" I sat up, wiping my mouth. I had been drooling. *Well, that's embarrassing.*

"You okay?" Cullen asked.

"Yeah, what time is it?" I sat up, trying to get my bearings.

"Almost 3."

"Bleep! I slept for an hour."

"Wow."

"Where's Noah?"

"He was talking to Smokes."

"Ah, okay." I started to stand.

"Can you wait a second, I have something for you." He swung his backpack from his back, then dug inside, pulling out a USB drive. "Footage from the hitman's murder."

"I don't want to see a murder." I'd already seen too many in my life.

"No, we can stop it before that."

"Okay."

I probably should have asked how he got it, but I knew he had a tech hobby. He'd helped me before with pulling footage from secure places. I figured the less I knew, the better.

He plugged it in the computer, then clicked around until the video pulled up.

"Ready?"

"No, but yes." I took a steadying breath.

It showed what looked like a mostly empty warehouse. Metal shelves on one wall, crates and equipment on another, but not much else. There was a roll-up door with a regular door next to it.

A man came into frame, but he kept his back to the camera. It was as if he knew where it was and intentionally kept his back to it.

The camera appeared to be too far away making the footage out of focus and hard to see details. This made it difficult to tell the man's height, but if I had to guess he was roughly six feet tall, maybe more based on the size of the metal shelves that he stood in front of. He had broad shoulders and a thin waist.

Despite not seeing his face, there was something familiar about him, but I couldn't quite place how or why. That scared me a bit, because it was possible I had met him already and didn't even know it.

The side door opened. It seemed to be dark out as the light seemed dim, maybe from a streetlight rather than the sun.

"Okay, here is the hitman," Cullen said.

"Yeah, that looks like the guy we saw in the other video, the one from the Spicy Fig."

"Yeah, but here you can see his face."

My blood ran cold as he came into focus.

"I've seen him before. Oh, my gosh, I saw him the day the twins were out of school. We went hiking and he passed us on the trail."

"What? Really?" He paused the footage.

"Yes, this guy. This one." I pointed. "I had taken the twins for a hike to burn some energy, and he passed us when we were almost finished. He didn't say anything, um, oh, just good afternoon and then kept going." Saying it had me second guessing my memory of the day. "I remember having a weird feeling as he walked by, but I thought maybe it was just a stranger near the girls. You know, like a mom instinct to protect them. Nothing more."

"I don't know anything about all that."

"Yeah, I never thought I would either, but here I am helping to raise two little girls and sort of a teenager."

"Are you going to tell Rafferty?"

"Do you think I should? This guy is dead already, so what can the police do?"

"But clearly, he was following you, right?"

My body felt numb as thought after thought hit me. That day could have ended so much differently.

"He must have followed us to the park. I had the girls. I never thought of them as being in danger. Just me. What if he had decided that was his chance?"

"But he didn't. The girls are safe and so are you."

"For now."

Noah came into the room. "What's wrong?"

"Why do you think something is wrong?" I tried to smile, but I knew I wasn't fooling anyone.

"You look like you might cry."

That's when tears started. I wasn't boo-woo crying, but I couldn't hold the tears back. They spilled over from the fear. Fear for myself, fear for my friends, and most of all fear for those little girls who have already been through so much.

Cullen filled him in on the footage all the way until I realized the hitman had passed us at the park. Hearing it again, I began to sob uncontrollably.

Noah put his arms around me. "It's okay. It's okay."

"But what's okay? There is still this guy out there," I pointed to the other man on the screen. "He likely has all the same information that the first one had. Plus, he has the added motivation that he doesn't want to die. I mean, one would assume."

They both shrugged in agreement.

My phone chimed that I'd received a new text message.

It was from a blocked number and showed a picture of the twins on the playground at school with a caption that read:

They're awfully cute little girls.

I began shaking.

"What? What's it say?" Noah asked.

I just handed him the phone.

"Holy sh ... um, wow! You need to call Upton or Raff or Roberts. Someone."

"Yeah, but first I need to get to those girls." I jumped up, grabbing my stuff and getting my phone from Noah. "Thanks, Cullen. Thanks, Noah."

"Let me know, Jess. Really," Noah said.

I paused at the door. "I will."

As I bolted out of the office and through the kitchen, people called out to me, and I just yelled my apologies. Cullen or Noah could explain. I just needed to get to that school.

Skipping the long pick-up line, I pulled right into the parking lot. Once I stopped, I jumped out then looked all around. There wasn't a suspicious vehicle that I could see. No tall, dark man lurking. Of course not. He wouldn't want to be seen.

I glared out across every inch of visible area, just in case he was watching. He needed to know, I wasn't scared, even though I was literally shaking with fear.

I walked to where the girls were. They were singing with one of their friends.

"Oh, Jess! You're here."

"Where is your car?"

"I parked in the lot today."

"Do you have another flat tire?" Ivy asked.

If I wasn't so desperate to get home, I would have laughed because I had just gotten it back from the police department. They'd given me the all clear that nothing else was wrong with it. Just that one bad tire.

"Um, no, I was just so excited to give you both hugs today that I couldn't wait until we got home."

They giggled as I wrapped them in my arms. They were okay, they weren't harmed, and I could see them. We would be okay, at least I hoped.

I carried them to the car, even though they were almost too heavy for me. I helped them buckle in then, shutting the door, I glanced around once more. Still nothing that looked out of place. The only parked cars were those in the parking lot or waiting in the pickup line.

I hopped in and started for home. My only comfort was that the officers should be arriving shortly if not already there to stand guard for the evening. They would be there until morning.

Ten minutes, Jess, it should only take you ten minutes to get home. Then you'll all be safe.

The girls chatted the whole time, and I tried to give the appropriate responses to each and every thing they said. However, my mind was racing as I watched every car, looking in each window of every single vehicle we passed. Even parked cars could be a threat.

Any car that followed behind us for more than a block became a suspect, a danger. I kept an eye on them in the rearview mirror until they were no longer behind us.

Someday, I hoped I could look back on this and laugh at myself for how quickly I had taken on a motherly role. It was surprising, but not funny at all today.

Our townhouse came into view, and I could see the officers were there. As I'd suggested, they had started to set up across from our unit in the empty one. At the moment, one of them was washing their car. It gave the appearance of normal suburban life without making it look like cops on a stakeout.

I breathed out a sigh of relief. *We made it home.*

"Okay, girls, inside. First one to the door gets to pick the snack!" I tried to make it sound fun so they could be quick. I should have known better.

"What if we tie again?" Ivy asked.

"Yeah?" Dove added.

Quick, Jess, you're smart. Think of something.

"Then, you each get to pick a snack." I looked around. "Okay? Ready, steady, go!"

They burst from the car with a ton of giggles as they tried to time their arrival at the door to be in sync. It was a win-win for all of us. I got the door opened quickly then we were in our home.

Letting out a sigh of relief, I turned to listen to the twins' requests.

"We want crackers with cheese and those little meat slices."

"Um, really?" I should never have introduced them to charcuterie boards. They have become obsessed, but today I was willing to give them anything, just as long as I could keep them safe.

"Yes, with grapes and strawberries and Shirley Temples to drink."

"Anything else, ladies?"

They exchanged a look, then shook their heads.

"Coming right up, but first, go get your homework and get started."

"Okay!"

They ran to drop their shoes and backpacks in their room, coming back with just their homework folders. Climbing onto the bar stools, they got right to work.

I busied myself with slices and chopped up their snack, including mixing their mocktail for them. I loved Shirley Temples myself but hadn't had one in years. Then on New Year's Eve, we had an early celebration with charcuterie boards and mocktail drinks. That's when I introduced this to the girls.

We did it again once for a movie night with them. They were now hooked. I had told them only for special nights but today felt special. They were safe. We were home. Nothing could get them here.

Chapter Eighteen

Later that night, everyone was in bed. I lay wide awake, which seemed to be my new normal, staring at the pictures on my wall. The elven boy had always been comforting to me, but tonight even he seemed to feel my anxiety.

I had gotten him from Flora who, along with three others, had tried to sabotage my business. But I didn't know that when I'd bought the picture from her.

Regardless, I loved the little elf child. He had a mischievous grin and a look in his eyes like if only he could talk, he'd tell me all his secrets. Luca was what I'd named him.

Next to him was a dragon painting that April, Colt's sister, had given me. It had been his and she said he would want me to have it. Colt had been a blind date I never got to go on. He was murdered on his way to meet me.

Then I had watercolors by Tilly Martin. She was a local artist who did landscape and architecture paintings from around Dashwood and the surrounding areas.

There were a few others, but those were my favorites. Usually they calmed me, but my heart pounded in my chest and breathing was difficult and painful.

Baxter came and stood on my chest, kneading his paws on me. It was as if he sensed what I needed right now.

"Aw, thank you, Baxter. Are you trying to comfort me?" If he didn't weigh a million pounds, it might have worked.

He began purring loudly, the sound rhythmic and hypnotic with the pressure and feel of his paws massaging me. I actually did start to calm. My heart slowed, my breathing became more even, and I slowly slipped to sleep.

I was startled awake hours later. Well, I didn't realize it was hours until I looked at the clock. What woke me? I sat up.

Vee came running in.

"Did you hear that?" she asked.

Shayla burst in wide-eyed, but before she could speak, she turned and ran downstairs. Her sisters were screaming and crying out for her.

"What's happening?" I asked.

"There was gunfire outside."

We ran to look out our one front window. It was downstairs between our front door and the kitchen. From here, we could see one of the officers was on the ground and the other was standing over him. It looked like he was performing first aid. There were faint sounds of sirens.

Vee and I slipped on shoes, and ran out to see if we could help. Plus, we needed to know what was going on.

"Stay in the house," Vee yelled back to Shayla.

We jogged across the street to the unit where the officers were. I could see the one down was Emerson and the one working on him was Blair. Lights were coming on in all the units on the streets and neighbors started to come outside to see what was happening.

"Is there anything we can do?"

"No, no. The ambulance will be here. You should go back inside your house, just in case they come back."

"What? Who?" A lump formed in my throat. Was this because of me? I looked around, suddenly realizing that this could be dangerous for Vee and me.

Officer Blair stood, blood dripping from his hands. "Please, go back in the house! Once the others get here, someone will come talk to you."

"Okay," Vee said, pulling me back.

Once we were safely inside, we watched from the window as an ambulance arrived followed by several squad cars. They worked on the young officer, but sadly we saw them pull a sheet over him.

Vee and I hugged. She started repeating a prayer over and over. I joined her, but in my head. I didn't trust my voice at the moment. That young man died because of me. Because I needed protection.

I looked out again, as they started working on Officer Blair. It looked as if he must have been shot, too.

"Oh, my gosh. I did this!"

"No, no, you didn't. Someone else pulled that trigger, you did nothing." Vee tried to assure me. "There might have been a burglar. Until we know more, don't beat yourself up."

"That's true." I was going to focus on that.

A couple of officers looked over at our house. One was Rafferty. I knew he was likely worried about us but had a job to do before he could ensure we were safe.

They began blocking off the street with tape, measuring, and collecting evidence. Officer Blair seemed to be okay as it looked like he was giving a statement. He gestured this way and then held his head when he looked over at his partner.

Even though I didn't know him well, I could feel his grief from here. He just watched his partner get gunned down and die in his arms.

Shayla came to join us.

"The girls fell back to sleep," she whispered. "Do we know anything yet?"

"Just that one of the officers was killed and the other looks to have been hurt as well," Vee said.

"Oh, no!" She clasped a hand over her mouth, then looked up at me.

I couldn't look at her, just continued to stare out the window.

We stood there for another twenty minutes before Upton and Rafferty finally came to our door.

"Are y'all okay?" Raff asked. He looked me up and down to make sure, I guess.

"We are," Vee spoke for us.

"And the girls?"

"Scared at first, but now sleeping. Sound asleep," Shayla said.

"Would it be better for us to speak outside?" Upton asked.

"Um, yes, that would be better. Thanks."

We followed them out. I still hadn't found my voice, but I knew I couldn't stay quiet forever. At some point, they would expect me to say something.

"Okay, so here is what we know so far," Raff said, looking at me. "A car came around the corner, no plates. Blair couldn't see who they were. They shot at them, before they could even react."

"And, unfortunately, Emerson didn't make it," Upton filled in.

I choked on a sob. Raff put his arms around me. That's when the tears and guilt spilled out.

"This is all my fault," I sobbed against him.

"No, it's not your fault. Not your fault at all." He rubbed my back as he held me tightly.

"I know it was the middle of the night, but did any of you see or hear anything leading up to this?" Upton asked us.

"I was asleep."

"Me too."

I simply wept.

"Can we see the footage from your camera?"

"Yeah, I have my phone." Vee pulled it out, navigated to the app, then pulled up the footage. "Here."

Upton watched it with Raff watching over my shoulder.

"It's just like Blair said. No plates and the car is hard to see."

"We need to see if others have better footage."

Rafferty looked at me, then over at Vee. "You got her?"

"Yes, give her to me." She took me around the shoulders as best she could.

We went back to our townhouse. Vee laid me on my side, then sat next to me and began stroking my hair. She reminded me to breathe in and out.

"In, one, two three, four, and out, one, two, three, four."

I followed her instructions. The tears stopped, but I felt no desire to speak. My only thoughts were how this was because of me, even if not my fault, it was indirectly.

"Do we stay awake?" Shayla asked.

"No, why don't you go to sleep. Someone will need to be ready for the twins in the morning," Vee said.

She nodded, then headed upstairs.

After Shayla left, I sat up. "Okay, this isn't my fault, but they wouldn't have been here if not for me, right?"

"Shh, don't think like that. Nobody, and I mean, nobody will blame you for this."

"You sure? What about his family?"

"They won't report details because that is private. They will only say killed in the line of duty."

"You're right. Still, I have guilt."

"Because you are such a caring person."

"It was that hitman. The new one."

"We still don't know that," she said.

"But we do. It was a targeted hit. They drove up, shot at them and drove off."

"I know, but in the bigger cities, cops are targets like that all the time."

"But this is *Dashwood*, not a big city," I choked out. "It had to be the new hitman. That means they know where I live."

Vee didn't respond. I guess she couldn't put a positive spin on that. I did appreciate her optimism about this, but I knew it was tied to Samir's case.

We sat there in silence, the blue and red lights from outside flashing around the dimly lit room. My phone chimed with a text.

"Raff wants us to come out."

She stood. We held hands as we went to the door. Upton, Roberts, and Raff were standing on the sidewalk.

"Okay, we will be out here for a while gathering evidence and to keep the scene secure. We wanted to let you know to go ahead to bed. Try to sleep," Upton said.

"Do you have any information for us?" Vee asked.

"Nothing really. Not the kind of information you want like the who and why. We only know what happened."

"Understood."

"And Roberts and I will be the ones standing guard after tonight," Raff said.

I gasped. "What if they come back?"

We had only just started our relationship. I couldn't risk losing him. We hadn't even said I love you, yet.

"I know what you are thinking, but I promise, we will be fine. I'll be fine." I looked at him, tears in my eyes. "Jess, I promise, you aren't getting rid of me that easily."

He wrapped his arms around me, as I gave a slight chuckle to his joke.

"We will likely still be here in the morning, but with a smaller presence," Upton said.

"Thanks," Vee said.

With nothing left to say, we headed back into our house. Vee went upstairs while I stood at the window for a moment watching. My heart ached for the loss, but I also had a new resolve to figure out who this was and put a stop to this.

Chapter Nineteen

I had tossed and turned all night. It was now morning, and I just laid there a minute staring at the ceiling. Last night, all I could think about was how I needed to solve this today. No more excuses. I needed to put my thinking cap on and try to piece together what I knew.

I swung out of bed, grabbing the murder board from the closet. I hadn't added anything to it in a while. It wasn't as convenient as it had been when we had it downstairs. But the twins deserved a room that was all theirs.

Since I didn't have access to any of the physical evidence, I had to go based on what I had seen and heard. Hence the board worked to list everything and then see it. Victim and their relationship to each person. Suspects and possible motives then linking those to each opportunity.

I added the salesperson, Mike, to the board. Following Shayla's lead on our last case, I wrote creepy under his name. He was creepy.

However, based on what my dad and Marisol told me, I knew that Avery West Equipment was the source of a lot of crime. He was a sales manager there, so it stood to reason, he was a suspect.

In fact, at current, he was my number one suspect, but I needed to look at all the facts.

Next, I added the dead hitman with his clues, like saw at park, killed Samir, burned down Zelda's. I didn't know his name or how he was associated with whoever it was that hired him. I'd never wanted to know, so I never asked or looked it up. Based on what I knew, I would almost bet it was via the Avery West company.

We do know that he killed both Samir and Zelda's employee, but I didn't know for sure that he was connected to Avery West. I should have researched that.

But that was what I needed to figure out. Where did the buck stop? Was it Klein, Avery West, or a higher level within this whole pyramid scheme they had going on?

Then I added Penny with her title at Klein. She told me it wasn't their company, but I still had doubts. Nobody would admit freely that they were bad guys, right? No, you would deny, point fingers, and deny some more. All of those things she had done.

Plus, Fatima's reaction to her. Fatima was normally a friendly, calm person, but when she spoke to Penny, her body language said they had a stressful relationship.

Then, Penny had confirmed their investments came with high fees because of this so-called protection they offered. That hadn't helped Samir or Zelda.

That made Penny a top suspect as well.

There was a knock at my door. I grabbed the poster board, shoving it under my bed as fast as I could.

"Come in."

"Good morning," Vee said, pushing open the door. "I thought I heard you moving around."

"Oh, good. It's you. I was worried it was the little girls." I pulled the board back out.

"It sounds like they are all still sleeping."

We had a rough night but thankfully it was Saturday, so they didn't have to be up anytime soon.

"I'm just trying to go through this. After last night, I just want this all to be over." I frowned down at the board. I couldn't remember what my next sticky note was going to be.

"Oh, can I help?" She shut the door behind her, climbing on to my bed.

"Yes, please. This is what I have so far."

She tapped one of the new sticky notes. "Mike? You didn't tell me about a Mike."

"I didn't? Darn, I thought I had. So much has been happening in such a short time and the twins are always around, it's made it difficult to discuss."

I went through everything with her. The visit with my dad and how he told me that all of those guys were pitted against each other. It still seemed strange to waste so many resources to divide them up. Not my decision on how they use their resources though.

Next, I told her about meeting Marisol and swore her to secrecy. Then all the way back to Tuesday when it seemed everyone was coming into the restaurant.

"When Penny and Erin came in, Fatima's face fell, and she kept her eyes down or on Mona. Penny went to say hi to her, but Fatima barely looked up."

"That's not like Fatima. She is always so friendly. I see her in the Post Office all the time. She sends letters, cards, and packages home to Lebanon all the time for her mother and sisters."

"Yeah, that's why Penny is a suspect with a capital S. She tried to point to the equipment leasing company as a problem, but I can't help but think some of it starts with her or at least Klein."

"What about the receptionist? Erin or whatever you said her name was."

"Why do you think her?"

"Receptionists know a lot of stuff. They normally have access to their bosses' calendars, hear a lot of private things, and see all the comings and goings of an office."

That gave me some pause. It made sense, but did I think she was the one?

I wrote her name and stuck it to the board.

"But I keep going back to what Marisol said about Samir wanting to break the contract and his threatening to go to the police. He said that to Penny."

"Then it has to be Penny, right?"

"Yeah, but Marisol also said that Stone, Upton, and Raff all know about that. If they didn't think it was enough evidence, then I can't just assume it."

"Can you talk to Fatima about Penny? Her relationship with Penny, I mean."

"That's a thought. See if she can shed light on their relationship and why Fatima pulled inward when Penny was there."

"Great. Let me know if you need a ride or die when you do." Vee stood. "Breakfast?"

"I'm coming. You want French toast or pancakes?"

"I think you know," Vee said with a laugh.

"Fluffy stack of pancakes coming right up."

I put the board back in the closet, then grabbed my cell phone.

A couple of hours later, Vee and I were seated at Roasted Beans waiting on Fatima to join us. She had been more than happy to talk to me. Malory's place seemed like the perfect neutral spot and we also knew that Mal wasn't part of whatever criminal element was happening in town.

Vee ate her lemon pound cake with a smile. I hadn't even touched the cranberry scone I'd ordered. I stirred the coffee in front of me and fidgeted with the fork.

Through the large windows, I could see Fatima getting out of her car.

"Here she comes," I said.

Then, I saw Anwar. My heart sank. Couldn't he have let her come alone? But perhaps she was nervous with everything going on. I stood as they came in the door.

"Jess, so good to see you." Fatima came, kissing my cheeks. "And Vee, so good to see you as well." She greeted Vee with kisses as well. "You both remember my son, Anwar, I'm sure."

"Yes, hello."

"Hi."

He nodded, but didn't speak.

"We'll just get our drinks and join you in a moment," she said.

"Of course."

"He's always *so friendly*," Vee whispered with an eyeroll.

"Yeah, isn't he?"

Minutes later, they joined with their Chai Tea. It smelled so heavenly with the spices that I was a bit jealous. Next time, I thought.

"I'm so glad you called when you did. I have the invitations for the grand reopening." She dug through her purse, pulling out two envelopes, sliding one each to Vee and myself. "Of course, you are both invited, and as I mentioned before, please bring Shayla, Ivy, and Dove."

"We will."

"Yes, we'll definitely be there."

"You wanted to talk about Penny," Fatima started. "There isn't much. I just don't trust her or anyone at Klein. They do dirty business. I also knew that they weren't happy when we pulled our business. Then through our new investor, we paid off the loan with them, so I have no reason to speak to her."

"Well, that makes sense, but … and I hate to ask, but I could tell you were uncomfortable around her. You didn't make eye contact and kept your body very still while she was talking with you," I said.

She looked at Anwar. He gave her a stern look which she returned. Clearly there was more here, but what, I didn't yet know.

"She called me right before we connected with the new investor. She was pressuring us to pay and had increased the late fees and added an administrative fee because we weren't bringing in revenue any longer."

"Well, that's not fair."

"Exactly. That's why we had to find this one."

"Who is the new investor?"

"Well, you know Garrett Majors?"

"Garrett? Garrett Majors is your new investor?"

Garrett Majors aka Chef Majors was one of the biggest names in celebrity chefs. He has won numerous awards, competitions, and hosted at least a dozen different cooking shows. I appeared on two of his competition shows. One was *Versus Majors* in which you face off with him. I won.

In fact, I had faced him several times over the years in various competitions, not just the twice on his shows, and I'd won all of them. He rarely lost competitions, so he held a grudge.

"That's right, you know him, don't you," Anwar said, a smirk across his face.

"Don't do that. It's rude," Fatima corrected. "Yes, Chef Majors. I'm sorry, Jess. I know you both have history, but he heard about us and was looking to expand. He said it was the perfect chance for him to not only help someone but expand into a new market."

Of course he wanted to expand here.

I simply smiled. "That's nice. He has good connections. I'm sure this will work out much better for you all."

"So far it has. He has reasonable terms for repayment and has left a lot of the decisions up to us. Not interfering at all. He simply wants to help us relaunch Samir's dream and brand."

That didn't sound like the Garrett Majors I knew, but again, I wasn't going to spoil things.

"That's wonderful. I'm so happy and I'm sure Samir would be so proud."

"I think so, too," she said. "Is there anything else you'd like to know?"

"You said Penny was pressuring you, did she make threats? Physical threats?"

"No, just said she would keep adding fees and if that didn't work, she'd take us to court. She never seemed violent." Fatima gasped, "you don't think she did this, do you?"

"Don't you?"

"I hadn't thought about it. Simply that she was a harsh businesswoman doing a job, a bad job, but still her job."

"Yes, that's probably all it is. I just have to gather information and after your encounter with her at my place, I wanted to check."

"Of course. I did ask you to look into this. I appreciate it so much." She looked over at Anwar. "However, I am at peace now."

"You are?"

"Yes, we will be opening the restaurant again soon, and I'm just ready to move forward."

"I can understand that. You have all been through so much," Vee said.

"Yes, I can understand your feelings."

"Well, we need to get going," she said, standing. "Thank you so much and it was good to catch up for a few minutes."

We hugged her goodbye. Anwar just stood back without a word, but he did throw a dirty look my way as they went out the door.

"Wow, what is his problem with you?"

"He must be a Garrett Majors fan."

"Ha, yeah, must be."

Chapter Twenty

The rest of the weekend went by without any shootings, flat tires, or threats. It was quiet. Well, if you don't count the squeals and laughter of busy eight-year-old girls.

They had a lot of questions about Friday night's chaos. Thankfully, Detective Upton, who was used to young children, was available to speak to them.

When he overheard their questions, he asked Shayla if he could speak to them.

"Of course. I have been trying, but I don't know what to say."

"The key is to not lie, but also don't give too many details," he had told her.

Once they had the scene mostly processed and removed all the barriers, which didn't happen until late Saturday afternoon, he came to speak with them.

"Do you remember me?"

"Yes, you are Detective Upton," Ivy said.

"You helped with mama."

"Yes, that's right."

"And you have two children," Ivy said.

"I do."

"They are still babies," Dove added.

"They are."

They met them once at a park. Evie was nearly a year old, and Aiden would be three soon.

"So, as you both know, the world sometimes has bad people in it. That's why we have police officers, to try to keep people safe. Sometimes that comes with danger. When our people tried to stop the bad guys, there were shots fired and that's what you heard."

"Were the police officers okay?"

"Sadly no. One was hurt and the other died."

"Like mama," Dove said.

"Yes, like her."

"That's sad," Ivy said. "Did he have kids like us?"

"No, he was not married and had no children."

They nodded and started asking him questions about Aiden and Evie. They wanted to play with them again.

"I'll talk to my wife and Shayla, and we will make some plans, okay?"

"Yay!"

That was it. They didn't need additional information and didn't mention it again. Thankfully, they would be starting their therapy soon so it was something they could discuss then, if they still had questions.

I pulled into the back parking lot of my restaurant just before eight. I liked being here a little early so I could enjoy a moment of peace before it got crazy.

Climbing out of my car, I noticed a white BMW parked at the eye doctor's office. I could tell there was a man inside, but he was parked too far for me to see his face clearly.

Oh, well, it must be for the doctor's office. They opened at eight for the day. They often had a car or two waiting on them.

After I got all the lights on and a pot of coffee going for the staff, I began prepping veggies for soups and the various side dishes. It gave me clarity. The rhythmic motion of the blade through each piece of vegetable. The onions flying, smashing the garlic, dicing carrots, I felt at home.

I could almost forget that there was still a hitman out there looking for me or that an officer had been killed right in front of my house.

People started to arrive, jumping right into their tasks. That's what I loved about my employees, they needed little direction and knew what was expected of them.

But something was nagging at me. We weren't open yet and since we were more or less ready for the day, I figured I deserved a break.

"Hey, I'll be right back," I told Eli.

I headed to the office. Noah wasn't in there, which gave me undisturbed time to review the security footage from when the two hitmen met and only one left alive.

I popped the USB in then clicked the video.

The second hitman came into view. I studied him from behind. I know I'd seen him before, but without a face, I couldn't be sure. After work, I would confirm my suspicion.

"Chef?" Eli stuck his head in. "It's time."

"Okay, be right there." I looked once more at the video before closing it and popping the USB back into my purse.

I went out to join the bullpen and start the long day.

"Special for the day," Eli read out to the staff before opening. "Cajun seasoned catfish filet topped with remoulade sauce on a bed of corn succotash and a house salad. Soup of the day is Minestrone. Any questions?"

"Nope!"

"Sounds good."

"Okay, Crock Potters, ready?" Skye yelled as she walked towards the front door.

"Yes!"

"Let's go!"

We all took our stations, but what happened next was unreal. There was a crash then the sound of gunfire from the dining room and screams mingling with the sound of a deep voice giving commands. The kitchen went silent.

"Everyone into the kitchen. Now!" A voice came from the dining room. "You lock the door, then follow me."

Suddenly, all of my front of house staff were filing into the kitchen and then sitting on the floor. A man in a mask followed closely behind them, shouting more orders and brandishing a gun.

"Cell phones in the middle! Now!" He looked around. "Don't try to call the police and nobody try anything."

I hit the panic button on my station. We had them installed after that group tried to sabotage everything. It wasn't obvious to anyone that it was even there. I mean who would expect a panic button in the kitchen? I just hoped he hadn't seen me.

Without even seeing his face, I knew exactly who it was. It validated my hunch from earlier. I figured I had time to talk to Detective Upton and Raff later today, but I supposed this guy had different plans.

"Hi, Mike," I said, as I came around my station to have a seat next to Ava. She was crying, so I wrapped an arm around her. "You're looking different than the last time I saw you."

"Shut up!" he growled out. "You don't know who I am."

He really thought his mask was working. Maybe to folks who hadn't spoken to him before, but he had introduced himself to me.

Trying to sell me equipment when my kitchen was brand-new and state-of-the-art, had sent up red flags in my mind. At that time, I had studied his face and watched him walk away. When I viewed the video earlier, I had known it was him.

Then seeing the car across the street, I hadn't gotten a good look at the driver, but he had a unique shape, broad shoulders with a thin waist, like a swimmer. It was the same as in the footage.

"Oh, but I do. I figured it out this morning, but it sealed it when I saw you sitting across the street."

He didn't say anything, just waved his gun from employee to employee as if counting them.

"You're smarter than the other guy. He let his emotions get the better of him, that's why you had to take over, right?"

"I said, shut up!" He came over snarling at me.

"They always say if you want something done right, you have to do it yourself, huh? Using selling kitchen equipment as an excuse to come talk to me, get a good look at me so you'd know that you got the right person, right?"

"You think you're just so smart." He whipped off the mask. "There? Happy? Yes, yes, it's me and I'm going to finish what that idiot couldn't do. Unfortunately, it will be at a higher cost than just you. Now I will be killing … umm, eight, twelve, uh, looks like sixteen people."

Some of the staff made whimpering sounds, some sucked in air, while a few were calmer like me.

"This is between you and me, Mike, why don't you let them go? Then we can talk?"

"Let them go? Ha, they have now seen my face thanks to you. So no, I won't be letting anyone go."

I looked around. Marco simply nodded. I think I know what he was thinking.

"How about this? Just let the girls and Arlo go?" Arlo was my oldest employee. It seemed like a fair request.

Mike looked around. "Not yet. I don't trust any of you."

"They'll leave their phones and promise not to call the police. Right, everyone?"

They all agreed.

"Fine. Only the girls and whoever this Arlo is." He pointed a gun at Arlo. "I assume that's you."

"Yes," Arlo mumbled.

"But if anyone calls the police, everyone else will be killed. You won't want that on your conscience right?" He waved the gun directing them. "Now, slowly one by one, and no cell phones."

Nobody moved. They looked over at me.

"Thank you, Mike. Alright, ladies and Arlo, please single file out the front door, lock it behind you."

But when Mike turned to watch them leave, I whispered to Ava not to lock the door. She gave a very slow nod as she followed the others out.

"Okay, now that it's just us, can we talk about this? Why are you doing it?" I asked, even though I did know why.

I thought if I could keep him talking, keep him distracted, it would give the police time to get here. I still can't believe he had agreed to let anyone go. He must not be the brightest criminal.

"Ha, I can't believe you don't already know. You are too nosy for your own good."

"Tell me anyway. I just want to hear it."

He turned slowly, then walked towards me as he spoke. "Because I can't have you messing up my business. You have too much power, success, and too many friends. You'll turn them all on me and I will have nothing. No business left. I've already lost the Spicy Fig and We Scream Ice Cream to Garrett Majors."

"Did you say We Scream Ice Cream?"

"Yes. Oh, you didn't know that Garrett Majors is helping Zelda?" He let out a wicked laugh. "Your rival is helping two of your 'friends' so that's gotta hurt."

It did, but I wasn't going to admit it out loud. However, it wasn't really the friends, but the fact Garrett couldn't let go of a little competition from years ago. He really did hold a grudge.

"There is plenty of business here for him and me." I tried to mean it. "Now, Mike, can we talk about some of my other employees? Maybe let a few more go. This really isn't between them and you, it's only between me and you."

He looked around at them. "Fine. You ... um, you, you, and you can go. Same rules apply. If anyone calls the police, these three die."

Great, just Noah, Marco, and me left behind. Of the people on my staff I would want to be in a hostage situation with, these were the two guys I would pick. We had brains and brawns here, so we were good until the cavalry showed up.

"So, what's the end goal here, Mike?" I asked.

He turned to face me. "I want to stop you."

"Okay, I'm stopped. Now what?"

"Not like this. This is just a bad day. I want you dead."

"That doesn't work for me. Can we talk it out?" I was going to fake the confidence I really didn't have and keep talking as long as I could.

"No, now keep quiet. Let me think."

He paced around mumbling to himself. I couldn't hear what he was saying, but I'm pretty sure it didn't make sense. The three of us just sat there quietly watching him. We didn't dare speak to each other in case he snapped.

Nobody had gotten hurt yet, I wanted it to stay that way.

Movement near the doorway of the kitchen caught my eye. It was Kyle Rafferty. He put a finger to his mouth for me to be quiet. I shook my head. He nodded his, but again I shook my head.

"Um, hey, Mike," I said.

He turned to face me snapping. "What?"

That gave the police an opening. Raff came in followed by Roberts and Blair. Upton brought up the rear.

"Put your weapon down, hands up," Raff said. His voice firm and loud. If I wasn't in a life and death moment, it would have been sexy as heck.

A gun went off, and a hot fire burned through me. I hit the floor.

"Jess!"

I don't know what happened after that as I think I passed out from the pain and shock. When I came to, there was an EMT next to me and I was sitting up.

"Jess, you okay?" a voice next to me asked.

I looked over. It was Marco. He was holding my hand.

"What happened?"

"That guy shot you."

"Oh, my gosh. Am I dead?"

"No, no. He just got you in the arm. You'll be fine. It looks as though it went right through. They are taking you to the hospital to have a better look and to get you patched up." He smiled. "You were a real hero today."

"I didn't do anything. Nothing more than anyone else would."

"But, nonetheless, you are a true hero."

The EMTs loaded me onto a stretcher and lifted it up. I could finally see around the kitchen area. Rafferty was across the space talking with Noah and Arlo. He saw me and a smile spread across his face. It was beautiful to see. When I would show up at crime scenes in the past, he would flash me one of those smiles, but now it meant so much more.

He came to stand next to me. "You okay?"

"Well, kind of. A bit loopy and I can't feel that arm much."

"They gave you some good meds." He kissed my head. "I have to finish up here, but I'll be up at the hospital as soon as I'm done."

"What about Ivy and Dove? I'm supposed to pick them up later."

"I've already called Vee. She's going to handle calling everyone else and picking up the girls. No need to worry about anything. Just rest and get better."

"And Mike?"

"We have him in custody. He isn't talking, but that's fine, I think we have enough evidence."

"Okay." I was getting light-headed, so I laid my head back again.

"Rest well. See you later."

With that the EMTs rolled me from the kitchen into the dining room. My staff were lined up on both sides of the stretcher's path. They cheered and clapped as I was rolled through.

"Thank you, Chef!"

"You're a hero!"

"Our hero!"

"Get better."

I tried to focus, but the pain medicine they were pumping into me via the IV drip was working. I closed my eyes and missed the entire ride to the hospital.

Chapter Twenty-One

It had been two weeks since I'd been shot, and my arm was still immobile, wrapped up and in a sling as it healed. The bullet hit my bone and tore some muscles, so it would likely be a while before I could use it again. The doctors were saying six to eight more weeks.

I didn't know if I could go that long without being able to cook. It was my stress reliever, my therapy, my joy, and my work. It gave me life. Now I was stuck working as a hostess and couldn't lift much, so I was limited to only carrying menus and talking to customers.

The staff were just so thankful to be alive, they didn't mind picking up my slack. They still kept thanking me and calling me a hero. I just did what needed to be done.

Everyone in town had rallied around The Crock Pot, bringing get well cards and sending flowers.

Mayor Patricia Lackland hosted a ceremony at city hall awarding me a certificate of bravery. It was embarrassing. They'd expected me to give a speech. What could I say?

"I just did what anyone would do."

The name of the crime-fighting chef had been put all over the city website and social medias sites, as well as the local news stations and newspapers. If anyone didn't know who I was and what I did, they sure would now.

Thankfully, tonight was the grand reopening of The Spicy Fig. My fifteen minutes of fame should be over now and the spotlight shift to the Saad family instead. I was happy to pass that torch as I hated being the center of attention.

I stared at the dress I'd bought to wear tonight. It was a long black maxi dress in a lightweight linen material that flowed nicely when I moved. It had cap sleeves and a simple neckline. The entire thing was slimming and looked amazing on me.

However, with my arm bandaged and in a sling, I wasn't sure how I was going to get dressed.

Tonight, even though this was about the Saads, it was also the first time in three years I would face my nemesis. As the investor, of course, Garrett Majors would be there. The town was in a frenzy over the celebrity chef's arrival today.

I was probably the only one in town who was not excited.

"Knock, knock," Vee said at my open door. She was dressed for the evening in an A-line skirt and lavender blouse. "Do you need help getting dressed?"

"Don't you look gorgeous, and yes, that would be so helpful. I can do shirts, but a dress, not so much."

"I'm glad I can help."

She lifted the dress, and I ducked down so she could get it over my head, then together we carefully wiggled it down. When it came to pulling my injured arm through, she held the sleeve as I tenderly moved my arm through.

"Ouch," I winced once it was in place. "I can't believe how sore it is still."

"You were shot in the arm just two weeks ago, what do you expect?" She laughed.

"True, but I'm still upset that I can't use it for weeks. A lot of weeks."

"It will go by in a flash."

She helped me smooth down the dress, ensuring it lay correctly. I never wore dresses, skirts sometimes, but not dresses. With how great I looked in this one, I was thinking I should get more.

"Can you help with the necklace, too?"

"Of course."

I leaned forward as she clasped the thin silver chain on me. It was Y-shaped with a drop pearl at the end. It hung perfectly to just above my cleavage. Modest, yet elegant.

Though with the sling, nobody would likely even notice the necklace.

I slipped into my silver shoes, then took a step back.

"What do you think?" I asked.

"Garrett Majors will be stunned speechless."

"Ha, that will be a first."

Now that we were ready, we headed downstairs. Shayla was just finishing with the twins' hair. They had long French braids with ribbon twisted in it to match the color of their dresses. Ivy in purple and Dove in a pale blue.

"Don't you two look adorable. So pretty," Vee cooed at them. They grinned and modeled for her.

"Wow, Shay, you look ... amazing!" I said.

She was in a long maxi dress, like me, but hers was youthful with ruffles from waist to hem and a sweetheart neckline. The sage green chiffon fabric was light and shimmery against her light skin.

A blush formed on her face at the compliment.

"Thanks. It feels strange. I've never dressed up like this before."

"Yeah, but also kind of nice," I said.

"I like it!" Ivy shouted.

"Me to!"

"Me three!" Vee laughed, causing the little girls to giggle.

"Well, I guess we should head out," I said.

"And Kyle is working security for Chef Majors?" Shayla asked as we made our way to the car.

Most of the police department had been tasked with patrolling and securing the roads so that Mr. Majors would not be inconvenienced or accosted in any way.

"Yeah, though we might still see him there."

As we drove over, traffic was heavy and the closer we got to the Spicy Fig, we could see that many streets were blocked. The streets were lined with parked cars and people were walking towards the restaurant.

"Samir would be so happy."

"Yeah, even if a lot of this hype is for your enemy."

"Enemy? Who is your enemy?" Ivy asked.

"Um, nobody. It was a joke," I said.

That was the last thing I needed was them telling Garrett that I thought of him as my enemy. It wasn't exactly like that. More of a healthy competitive rivalry. At least that's what I was telling myself as we inched along.

We could see the restaurant in the distance. There were huge balloons with long streamers and a couple of colorful spotlights shining, though it was still daylight out. Music was pumping all the way to us from what I could only imagine must be the local radio station's mobile DJ.

"Wow, this is a big event," Vee said.

"Look at the balloons!"

"And the lights."

"All the people."

My passengers were excited, but dread was settling in my stomach. We were running late, and I hated that.

With our invitation to this, we were supposed to have valet parking so all we had to do was get close enough to get to the valet, but between the cars and pedestrian traffic, we weren't making good time.

Then a familiar face came into view. It was Officer Blair. He saw me and waved.

"Shouldn't you already be there?" he asked when I got even with him.

"Yes, but," I pointed in front of me.

"Let me see if I can help a little bit."

He pulled out a bullhorn and started directing people out of the way. He walked with us for a bit, until most of the traffic had cleared. He waved as we sailed on, pulling up to the valet station a moment later.

The porter took the keys and car, then we made our way to the red carpet. Yes, they had a red carpet for invited guests to walk. Barriers were holding back onlookers who were hoping to catch a glimpse of a celebrity or two.

"Chef Jessica!" People started shouting.

"Oh, and that's Chef Shayla!" a couple of young girls yelled.

Shay turned to me with a huge grin and a red glow on her face. She waved to the girls and went over to take a selfie at their request.

Ivy and Dove clung to Vee but giggled as they walked along.

"Our sister is famous," Ivy said to Dove.

Dove nodded and stared at the crowd with wide eyes.

I got called for a few autographs and selfies, too. Something I hadn't done in a long time. It was strange, but I had to admit, it was fun.

We finally reached the end of the red carpet where the Saad family was stationed to greet all the guests.

"Oh, Jess!" Fatima rushed over to hug me. "You made it. Isn't this amazing?"

"It is so amazing. Samir would be so proud."

"He would." She beamed as she greeted the rest of our party. "Please go in. Your table is all reserved."

The restaurant was less crazy. Seating was limited to invited guests. The hostess got us seated and handed us the special event menus.

"Smart that they have a set menu," I said.

"Look, Dove, that's Anya! Hi, Anya!" Ivy waved to her friend a few tables over.

Anya squealed and waved to them.

"This is so amazing," Vee whispered to me after we'd ordered.

A few diners came to take selfies with Shayla and me, gushing about how they loved our food.

"I go to Honey's all the time just to get one of your eclairs!" a diner said to Shayla.

"And your alphabet soup is amazing!" Another said to me.

After they left our table, Shayla turned to me. She had the biggest grin on her face.

"Is this what being a celebrity is like?"

I nodded. While I hated being the center of attention, I did like being recognized for my food and cooking abilities.

We were eating when there was a commotion outside with camera flashes, shouts, and cheers. A murmur went through the entire restaurant. People started to crane their necks to see what was happening, though we all knew who was causing the chaos.

"Must be Garrett," Shayla said, as she stretched in her seat to see.

"We don't like him, right?" Ivy asked.

"I don't," Dove announced.

I had no idea what to say. Do I lie to them?

"Girls, it isn't polite. We're friendly and nice to everyone," Shayla corrected.

They nodded.

I would need to remember that. My stomach was flip-flopping at the thought that any moment he would burst through those doors. I moved the hummus around on my plate as we waited and just kept my head down.

Then the murmurs started around the room again.

"He's coming!"

"Look!"

"Oh, my gosh!"

"Hello, Spicy Fig diners!" Garrett Majors had arrived. "Hello, all. Thank you for coming out to support my newest endeavors and of course, the wonderful Saads." He pointed at them. "They are a dream to work with."

He continued but my ears were ringing.

"And there she is, Chef Jessica! The only chef that I couldn't seem to beat." He came over to our table, clapping me on the shoulder. I winced. People close by gasped. "Oh, gosh, I'm so sorry. I heard you'd gotten shot. I forgot. My bad."

"It's okay, Chef Majors," I said through gritted teeth.

"And this young darling must be the newest winner of the little competition. Chef Shayla, right?"

Her cheeks turned three different colors of red, but she squeaked out a yes.

"Wonderful. I heard so many good things about your eclairs and your baking in general. I will be coming to try them soon. You're over at Honey's Sweet Treats now, right?"

"That's right."

"Couldn't live in the shadow of Chef Jessica forever!" He chuckled. I wanted to punch him.

"Um, I ..." Shayla stared over at me.

"I'm joking, darlin', just joking!" He threw his head back again to laugh. "And you, lovely dear, are you a chef, too?" he asked Vee.

"No, not me. I burn scrambled eggs. I leave that to the experts."

"Ah, I bet you aren't that bad."

"No, she *is* that bad," Ivy said.

Always the one to speak up and say what's on her mind. We all laughed at her truth telling.

"Well, aren't you the cutest doll. Are you going to be a chef?"

"Yes, Dove and I are both learning from the best two chefs in all of Dashwood. My sister and Chef Jess."

Dove grinned as she nodded her agreement

"Well, that's wonderful. I love hearing about young chefs."

Someone across the room called his name, he waved to them and then said goodbye to us. He quickly left our table, and that was it. It was over.

I breathed a sigh of relief. That reunion went about as I expected, except for him hitting my hurt arm. That was a bit aggressive.

"That was rude that he hurt you. I see why you don't like him," Ivy said as she watched him make the rounds.

A few hours later, we had said goodbye to the Saads and were standing in the parking lot waiting on my car. Garrett caught up to me. He signaled a camera over.

"So, Chef Jessica, now that I am going to be spending time in town from time to time, I wanted to challenge you to another cook-off. You game?"

"Um," I looked at the camera and at the crowd that was forming around us. What could I say? "Yes, I'll take that challenge."

"Well, alright! How about at the upcoming Art Festival in about a month. I'll be back around that time to help Zelda with the reopening of We Scream Ice Cream, and I was thinking about a booth out there anyway."

"What's the food?"

"You pick."

"I had planned to make gumbo, how about that?" Then I wouldn't have to change my plans.

"Gumbo? Well, okay, gumbo challenge it is."

We shook hands as the crowd cheered around us. Chanting varied between him and me. I smiled until the camera turned, then let my face fall once the spotlight was off of me.

What did I just get myself into? I didn't want to compete with Garrett again, but I guess some grudges never went away.

THE END

Before you go: If you loved Falafel and Fatalities, be sure to visit my website to sign up for my newsletter (if you haven't already) and to stay up to date on new releases and other bookish things.

When signing up, you will receive **Chef Jessica's Alphabet Soup Recipe** as a free gift. I have "had" it; it is yummy. (Okay, so obviously, it is my recipe, but still, I recommend it!)

Continue to the next section for this book's recipe!

Also, check out my other books! You can find links on my website.

www.ejwheltonwrites.com

Recipe:

I love chickpeas. Either added to a salad or mixed into hummus or fried up as a falafel. This recipe is a fairly standard one that you can find all over the internet. I didn't try to put my own spin on it, as these are just so good this way.

Ingredients:

- 1 can of chickpeas, 15.5 oz (rinsed, drained, and dried)
- 1 onion (roughly chopped)
- 3-4 garlic cloves
- 2/3 cup chopped fresh parsley
- 1/2 cup chopped cilantro
- 1 teaspoon salt
- 2 teaspoons cumin
- 1 teaspoon ground coriander
- 1 teaspoon baking powder
- 4 Tablespoons chickpea flour, all-purpose flour or almond flour (more or less any type of flour you prefer)

1. Pulse onion, garlic, herbs, spices in a food processor.
2. Next, add chickpeas, pulse a few times until combined (but not mushy or pureed)
3. Next, mix in baking powder, flour.
4. Place the tray in the fridge for about an hour to let the mixture set.

Pan fry method:
1. Add a couple of inches of oil to a large skillet with tall sides then heat over medium heat.
2. When the oil is heated, add the falafel balls to the skillet by lowering them gently into the hot oil. Leave space between the balls so they cook evenly.
3. Cook the falafel on the first side for about 30-60 seconds. Don't touch them. You don't want them to fall apart.

4. The falafel is ready to be flipped when the sides have turned a golden color.
5. Flip the falafel and cook on the second side for 30 seconds before removing them from the skillet to a paper towel-lined tray.

<u>Air fry method</u>:

1. Preheat air fryer to 350°F.
2. Spray falafel with oil, air fry for 14 minutes, flipping halfway, until golden brown.

Author note:

I hope you have enjoyed Falafel and Fatalities! I know I say this every time and it is always true. I had so much fun writing this one.

But I will admit it was also a struggle. At the time I wrote this, I had a lot of stress and struggles in my life, which makes the completion of this one so sweet and satisfying.

I'm really looking forward to writing Gumbo and Grudges. The last chapter of this one sets up the tone for the next book, so I hope you're excited.

And I can't wait to share the gumbo recipe with you. It was the one my own grandfather used. He rarely cooked, but he did make gumbo. I found it mixed in with some of my grandmother's recipes and I couldn't believe how lucky I was to have it.

However, at the time this is being written/published, I do plan to take a short break so I can get my life together. Ha! But the characters are all shouting in my head so I will be back as soon as I can.

Until the next book, happy reading.

www.ejwheltonwrites.com